Read the other exciting books in the
Fire-us Trilogy

TRILOGY: BOOK 2

JENNIFER ARMSTRONG AND NANCY BUTCHER

HarperCollins*Publishers*

Library of Congress Cataloging-in-Publication Data

Armstrong, Jennifer.

The keepers of the flame / by Jennifer Armstrong and Nancy Butcher.

p.　cm. — (Fire-us trilogy ; book 2)

Summary: After a virus destroys most of the world's adult population, a group of children are delighted to discover a colony of adult survivors in a Florida shopping mall, but soon find that they are not as friendly as they appear.

ISBN 0-06-008049-3 — ISBN 0-06-029412-4 (lib. bdg.)

[1. Survival—Fiction. 2. Science fiction.] I. Butcher, Nancy. II. Title.

PZ7.A73366 Ke 2002   2002020700

[Fic]—dc21   CIP
                                                                         AC

1 2 3 4 5 6 7 8 9 10

❖

First Edition

For Katie, Jon, and Niles
—J.A.

For Ken Siman
—N.B.

Where did Fire-us come from? Why did it take away all the First Mommies and First Daddies? We tried to be good. We tried to remember Manners and everything. We studied our Baby-Sees and looked both ways. Why did this happen to us?

—*The Book, page 64*

Chapter One

Cory stood spear straight, with her arms out from her sides and
her chin lifted. She had a limited view through the open
doorway, but every time she tried to shift to see around
the corner, get a different angle, one of the women tut-
tutted or snapped, "Stand straight. No fidgeting," and
she had to resume her awkward, uncomfortable pose. So
she had to be content with the view she had: the atrium
of the mall with its holiday village display, the false snow
glistening on the roof of Satan's workshop, the imps
poised with hammer raised or saw pulled back, ready to
do the devil's work. The setting sun streamed in through
the skylights and the great glass wall of Entrance West,
casting everything in the reddish glow of hellfire. From
where Cory stood on the carpeted footstool in Danielle's
Bridal Shoppe the dust and dirt mingled with the fake
snow was invisible.

"Isn't she going to be beautiful?"

"I'm so proud. My heart's beating like crazy!"

Cory's arms jerked, almost of their own will, and she
winced as a pin jabbed her shoulder blade.

"Corinthians 1:19, hold still. By the Flame, you're so
twitchy!"

"Sorry."

Casting her eyes down, Cory looked at the heads of the
three women circling around her, watched them turning
up the hem of the white gown, pinning darts along her

waist, tucking and gathering. They were like . . . she searched her memory. They were like construction workers welding together a steel building. That was what she felt like: rigid, welded, immovable.

"Most girls are so honored they hold perfectly still, as though being Chosen had turned them into precious statues," Proverbs 3:21 remarked. She tipped her face up to give Cory an admiring look. "Which is what you're going to be. A beautiful, precious statue—"

"Or a vessel," mumbled Exodus 21:2 around a mouthful of pins. "That's really more like it."

Proverbs 3:21 beamed up at Cory, and her eyes had a thirsting, almost beseeching light. "That's right, a vessel. Did your Visioning show you how wonderful it would be? Your destiny?"

"Well, I'd have to say—" Cory began.

"Of course it did!" Psalm 12 interrupted from behind Cory's legs. "They always do!"

"And what did you see, exactly?" Proverbs 3:21 urged, her expression becoming even more avid.

Cory used Psalm 12's impatient hand on her back as an excuse to turn her face up again and break eye contact with the women.

Her Visioning had shown her—darkness, confusion. Cory was still baffled and unhappy about it. She couldn't bring herself to admit to anyone that it wasn't the Visioning they all seemed to expect her to have.

It was supposed to have been a simple thing. At least, that was how it was explained to her before she left the Crossroads for her journey to East Florida Precision Industrial Lenses. First came the long, empty-handed walk in the sun down Highway 201 to the factory, where she was to fast, pray, meditate, and ask for her Visioning. For a few hours, at least, it had seemed exciting, exalting, almost beautiful. The strange ricocheting light that bounced around inside the factory as the sun moved across the sky shot fire into the lenses, breaking the light into rainbows.

Then the night had come, and with it the hunger and thirst. But even then, Cory had kept true to her training and stayed on her knees and tried to rededicate her heart. Whenever she felt herself tiring or wanting to lie down or thinking of foolish things, she forced herself to pray even harder. No water, no food, no sleep: that was the only way to purify the body and spirit enough to allow the Visioning to happen.

When the sun had risen, filling the factory with light again, it wasn't so beautiful and exciting anymore but painful. Cory had cried some, and doubted, but continued her vigil. Visioning would never come to a frivolous heart, and without Visioning, she would never know her path.

Pain is woman's lot—she had been told that countless times. So she had acknowledged the pain, laid down her weapons, and let it come in.

At last, on the third night, the Visioning happened. Cory wasn't aware of the moment when she had passed from this world into the Visioning. Maybe she had been walking around inside the factory without realizing it, and at first she thought she had wandered outside.

The road was dark, and the landscape was flat and shadowed. There was no line between the sky and the ground. There was no horizon. There was only the road Cory walked down. Often, she stubbed her toe against something in the path or tripped over some hard obstruction like a rock, but every time she tried to look directly down, her sight was obscured by some filmy material, like gauze, and it shifted and folded before her eyes so that she couldn't make out what she was walking over. Nothing grew at the sides of the road, but something like brambles kept snagging her long dress. It was exhausting, as though the road pitched steeply upward instead of running flat and straight into the featureless horizon.

As she continued forward, the snags became more frequent, and she stumbled more often than not on the stony path. If only she could see what was there! And then something seemed to pass over her head like a heavy downbeat of wings, and a voice said, Take off the veil.

Cory put her hands to her face. She was covered with layers of gauze, and she tore at it, layer after layer shredding in her hands as she hurried onward.

The rocks in the path were bones and grinning skulls. This was what she had been stumbling over, and what her dress had been catching on. Panicked, she looked up. She had come to a crossroads, where another path met hers at right angles. Her path continued on to the empty horizon, and the other path stretched away, left and right, in shadow.

Which way? There's no sign? Her voice was thin and tired.

But there was a sign. Now she saw that at the crossroad there was a signpost, with arrows pointing down each path, four ways. A great bird, an enormous brown owl, sat clutching the crosspieces with its scaled *talons. It regarded her with fierce yellow eyes and shifted from foot to foot. Cory could see every one of its feathers, down to the tufts at the owl's ankles and the tiny feathers fanning out from around its eyes.*

Did you speak to me before? Cory asked.

The owl turned its head slowly, looking down the path to the left; then it turned to look to the right and then down the path Cory had been trudging along. At last it turned its head back to Cory and spoke:

This is your path, it said, and with an audible rustle of its feathers, spread its wings wide, and it was an open book. Frightened, exhilarated, Cory stepped forward. A book! A real book! She grabbed the edges of the covers, trying to draw it closer, even though she was frightened of the owl. But the writing was impossible to make out, like the random tracks of sandpipers on a wet beach.

I can't read this! Cory cried out. What does it say?

And her Visioning was over. Cory found herself gripping the sides of a lens-grinding machine, with moonlight pouring down through a hole in the roof. She thought she heard wingbeats, but it might have been the wind.

By the time she had returned to the mall, Cory had decided not to tell anyone what she had seen. She didn't seem to have had the kind of Visioning everyone expected her to have, and she didn't want anyone to think she was different, by the Flame! So she said the kinds of things girls usually said when they went for their Visioning and tried to be vague about details. But it was as if a veil had been lifted, and now she looked at her life with new eyes. Doubt—her life was all doubt now.

As Psalm 12 worked her way around the wide hem of Cory's dress, and the other two women fussed and fiddled with the buttons running down the back and made admiring remarks about Cory's heavy blond hair even though the braid was in their way, there was a commotion out beyond Cory's field of vision. Something was happening outside Entrance West, a gathering of people, as Cory could see by the long, monstrous shadows thrown all the way down into the atrium from the setting sun outside. There were noises: a faint sound of the horses and chariot wheels, and a confusion of voices. Cory tightened every muscle in her body, straining to be taller, see farther.

"Corinthians 1:19, you're making this impossible!"

"I'm sorry," she muttered. "But something's happening."

Proverbs 3:21 stepped around in front of her with a beatific smile. "That's right. You're becoming a woman. I am so happy for you."

Teacher knew Teddy Bear was afraid. The others seemed to think the horses were wonderful, especially Action Figure, who was still perched on top of the reddish horse that pulled one of the chariots and yelling "giddyup, giddyup"—such a strange word for him to remember. But Teddy Bear was still so shaken by their dangerous journey up the river, with alligators surfacing alongside the boat like rotten logs—that with the big, snorting animals so close he was visibly shaking.

And no wonder! All these Grown-ups! Teacher realized she was shaking, too, still not over the shock of seeing real Grown-ups for the first time in—was it really five years? They were real Grown-ups, not just ghosts, not dreams, not pictures in her heavy scrapbook. And there were dozens of them, milling around, exclaiming over the children—over Mommy, Hunter, Teacher, and Angerman, who were the big kids, and the little ones, Teddy Bear, Action Figure, Baby, and Doll and the littlest ones, Puppy and Kitty who didn't even know how to talk like people. The women and men were picking up the little ones, carrying on about what a miracle it was, how extraordinary, a divine providence, while Ruth Tooten, the lady they had first seen on the beach where they ended their river journey, smiled and laughed and accepted congratulations as if she had created the kids out of thin air.

"Where have you come from? How long have you been alone? All this time? Since the beginning? And have you been taking care of yourselves? How did you get here? All by yourselves?" The questions came from every side, from men's voices and women's voices, such a strange sound.

Teacher could feel Teddy Bear trembling, pressing himself against her and staring wide-eyed at the press of big people. She nudged him behind her and then backed step by step out of the midst of the crowd until they were pressed up against the wall of the building. It was a big mall, a giant one. She remembered malls, full of shops and things to eat and electric games. She held The Book against her chest like armor, shielding her little brother.

Mommy and Hunter and Angerman were in the thick of things, still standing by the three chariots that had brought them from the beach where they had met Ruth Tooten and the other ladies, Romanzine and Galoshes, or something like that. Action Figure, his wild, bleached hair in clumps all around his head, sat bare chested astride the red horse, his ribs showing under his tanned skin.

"Come on down from there, son," one of the men said, and reached for Action Figure.

Action Figure growled and would probably have tried to get the horse to run, but the people were too densely packed around him, and one large man reached up and plucked the boy right off. Action Figure kicked, but the man set him down on the ground with a thump.

"They're half crazed and starved," the Romanzine woman exclaimed. "Poor things."

Mommy looked from one face to another. "But we're okay," she said. "We've taken good care of—"

"I'm sure you've done the best you could," Ruth Tooten said, putting one hand on Mommy's shoulder.

Teacher thought she saw a red flush on Mommy's face, but it might have been the deep glow of the sunset. Hunter stood foursquare beside Mommy with a look on his face that was half defiant, half relieved. And Angerman—his face was a mask. He had no expression at all. In the backpack he wore, the head and torso of his beat-up mannequin, Bad Guy, was like another head looking over his shoulder. Bad Guy's scarred face had more expression than Angerman's at the moment. *Don't Let a Little Rain Spoil Your Day*, Teacher recited to herself. It was one of the Ten Commandments.

"We've been traveling for a long time," Hunter said, raising his voice to be heard. "Weeks and weeks, maybe."

"From Lazarus," Mommy added. She reached out

and pulled Puppy and Kitty close to her, and they buried their faces against her legs. "It's south of here. That's where we've been living since—since it all happened."

Ruth Tooten was shaking her head in amazement. "What made you decide to leave?"

"Well," Mommy began. "We—I mean, me and Hunter and Teacher—were there and then—"

"And it just seemed like time to be moving on," Angerman broke in. "So we hit the road and here we are. We've been looking for a place we could start a farm, maybe."

Teacher gripped The Book tighter. He was telling it wrong. After Fire-us, when all the Grown-ups died and then so many kids starved or hurt themselves or got killed by wild animals, she and Mommy and Hunter lived with the little ones all by themselves in Lazarus. And *then* Angerman arrived—just a little while ago—and insisted they leave home and go find President. And they caught the wild stray children, Puppy and Kitty, who had to be captured like animals. She had it all recorded in The Book, their most precious thing, the thing that reminded them of their lives and of what it meant to be real. Why wasn't he telling it right?

"See, we were looking for—" Hunter started to say, when Angerman broke in again.

"And you're the first people we've seen," he said. The sleeves of his dirty camouflage shirt were rolled up past his elbows, and he stood with his hands on his hips, perfectly at ease with a group of Grown-ups.

Baby tugged on his elbow, and he bent down, his curly dark hair flopping over his face while she whispered in his ear. He stood up again. "And what we want to know is, Baby reminds me, how come you're not dead like all the other Grown-ups?"

In the startled silence that followed, Teacher noticed a girl her age slip out the door and stand at the edge of the crowd in the parking lot. She had long blond hair in a single braid down her back, and she strained to see Angerman and the others through the sea of bodies in front of her. She was hastily buttoning a red plaid shirt, as though she had just gotten dressed.

The one called Ruth let out a cheerful laugh that broke the tension. "Some of us were immune—we didn't get sick—and we've been living here ever since," she explained with an airy wave of her hand. "You children must be very brave to have taken care of yourselves so long."

Teacher saw Hunter bridle at the word *children*, and wanted to remind him of all the brave and responsible things he had done over the last five years, being their hunter, the one who went out into the wilderness to find cans of tuna, boxes of powdered milk, or medicine. Her head was hurting her with the effort of remembering everything she was seeing. She yearned to have some peace and quiet so she could write it all down and consult The Book. Sure, they had left Lazarus looking for President, hoping to get to Washington and find a Grown-up who could maybe explain why Fire-us happened, and make things right. But somehow, finding a whole group of Grown-ups living in a big mall was absolutely the last thing she had ever expected. Teacher shifted her grip on The Book and noticed the girl with the long braid circling the outskirts of the crowd, maneuvering close to where Teacher and Teddy Bear were. The girl's attention was on Mommy and Angerman and Hunter, however, and she didn't seem to notice Teacher standing with her back against the sun-warmed stucco wall to the left of the entrance.

Then Teddy Bear moved, his sneakers scraping on the cracked blacktop paving. The girl turned, and seemed to focus on Teacher, to notice her for the first time. Their eyes met, and Teacher found herself being scrutinized with a ferocious intensity. Then the girl's gaze dropped to The Book, and an obvious shock went through her. With an almost terrified look on her face, she raised her eyes again, and Teacher saw her looking up at the wall above her head. The girl's throat jerked as if she were choking on words that she couldn't get out.

Puzzled, Teacher looked up and over her own shoulder. In big, blocky faded red-plastic letters on the stucco wall was a sign that said THE CROSSROADS. She looked back again, holding The Book up before her with both hands in an unconscious gesture of self-protection.

The girl took a faltering step closer and stretched out one hand. Her breath was coming in ragged gasps, as if she had been running. But then the crowd began to surge toward the huge glass doors of the mall and swept the blond girl away from Teacher and Teddy Bear and The Book.

Chapter Two

Ruth Tooten led the group into the Crossroads Mall. Angerman hesitated at the entrance, not wanting to follow. He gazed at the glass doors, at the neatly painted white words on them: STORE HOURS MONDAY–SATURDAY 10:00–9:00, SUNDAY 10:00–6:00. NO SOLICITATION ALLOWED! Ahead of him, Hunter and Action Figure, Teacher and Teddy Bear, Mommy and Baby and Doll trooped inside after Ruth and the other Grown-ups.

"Look at our big new house!" Doll was saying to her dolly.

"It's as big as a princess castle!" Baby added.

Puppy and Kitty started to bound through the doors after Mommy. But Angerman grabbed their hands and pulled them back. They flinched and stared up at him, their brown eyes wide.

"Hold on there, kids, wait up for me!" he said, forcing a smile.

Puppy and Kitty blinked at him and said nothing. They had been with the family for several weeks now, but they still hadn't spoken a word. Just the occasional barks and meows, and that was it. Angerman wondered, not for the first time, what was wrong with them. Sometimes he thought he knew, but then his mind would run away from knowing it . . . five years old . . . and the New—the New—He felt his chest tighten with love and protectiveness toward them—and fear—for these children whom he had known only for a short while, these children who were so damaged.

Yeah, like you're the poster child for mental health, Bad Guy whispered in his ear.

"Shut up," Angerman snapped. He let go of Puppy's hand for a minute and twisted around to reach Bad Guy, who was riding in his backpack, jammed in with the empty picture frame that he used as a TV screen. Bad Guy was just a head and torso and arms now, ever since Angerman had yanked his legs off and tossed them into the river while the family was making their way north to Jacksonville. Good riddance.

Angerman snaked his fingers around the back of his neck. He found Bad Guy's smooth, plastic head and whacked it, hard.

Ouchies! Bad Guy protested. *Yowza! Is that any way to treat your old—*

"I said *shut up*," Angerman hissed. "You want me to throw the rest of you into the river, turn you into alligator bait?"

He could feel his face growing hot. Muttering under his breath, he reached down and grabbed Puppy's hand again. The twins blinked at him, looking frightened.

Just relax, Angerman told himself, and forced another smile. "Okay, we can go inside now. I just had to . . . adjust things back there."

The three of them proceeded into the mall after the rest of the family and Ruth and the others. There was a big, open hallway with shiny wooden benches. Late afternoon sunlight streamed through overhead skylights.

To the left was a wide doorway with a sign over it: CINE-THEATER 6. To the right were several stores, also with signs: EXPRESS HAIR SALON; THE PORTRAIT GALLERY; TUX CONNECTION; A STITCH IN TIME; WIX 'N' STIX THE PLACE FOR CANDLES.

Angerman was confused for a moment. Mall . . . that was something outdoors, with lots of grass and flowery trees and pretty buildings all around it. But maybe it was an indoors thing, too. This one certainly was.

Men and women passed by, casting curious glances their way. Grown-ups . . . it was so weird to see Grown-ups after all this time. They were so tall. Some of the men had hair on their faces, not just on top of their heads. The women had grown-up chests under their tunics.

That girl from outside—the one in the khaki pants and plaid shirt—was lingering near Teacher, checking her out. Who was she, anyway? Why was she so interested in Teacher? Angerman noticed that she had kind of a chest, too, under her shirt, even though she didn't look any older than Mommy or Teacher.

Ruth had stopped just outside the Cine-Theater 6 entrance and was smiling at the family. "This is where we have our nightly meetings. We'll have one tonight, and you're welcome to join us. Why don't I show you the rest of the mall now? Later, we can join the other Keepers at the Food Court for the Communal Evening Meal."

She continued to walk, and the others followed.

"Keepers?" Angerman muttered.

Jeepers, creepers, where'd you get those Keepers? Bad Guy sang out.

Angerman was about to whack Bad Guy again when he saw Mommy doubling back toward him and the twins. "Hey, hi," she said in a quiet voice. "Are you okay?"

"Fine and dandy!" Angerman replied. Puppy and Kitty wriggled out of his grasp and ran over to Baby and Doll, who were checking out the Earring Pagoda.

"Why'd you keep interrupting?" Mommy asked him. "When we tried to tell the Grown-ups about how we're looking for President, I mean?"

Angerman glanced at Ruth and the others, who were just ahead of them. Ruth was saying something to Teacher, who was nodding *yes yes yes*, like she was really interested in whatever Ruth was talking about.

"We don't really know these people," Angerman said. "We don't know anything about them."

Mommy looked surprised. "They're Grown-ups. Isn't that what we wanted to do—find some Grown-ups? They're big, smart people, and I bet you they remember all about the Before Time. They can help us."

"Or not."

Angerman didn't want to tell Mommy what was really on his mind. It was the image of the pale-gray horse, the one he'd seen on the side of the bridge in Jacksonville. As soon as he saw it, he knew it was a sign. And not a good sign, either, but a sign that something very, very bad was happening.

Who knew if the horse was connected to this mall? Or if the horse was connected to something else altogether? Either way, he didn't trust this Crossroads bunch. They gave him the creeps.

"Mommy, Mommy, lookit!"

Baby was shouting at Mommy from a display at the intersection of two halls. The display consisted of an enormous gingerbread house, candy canes the size of trees, a sleigh with reindeer, elves, and a fat Santa dressed in red. There was a ragged banner over the display that read MERRY CHRISTMAS, only the *mas* was crossed out, and somebody had changed the *e* to an *a*. MARRY CHRIST.

"Mommy, it's Santy Claus!" Doll shrieked, jumping up and down. "He's gonna give us Kistmas presents!"

"That's right, honey!" Mommy said, waving.

The little ones—Baby, Doll, Puppy, Kitty, Teddy Bear, and Action Figure—all ran into the gingerbread house, shrieking and laughing. Mommy watched them, her eyes shining with pleasure.

"What is wrong with *this* picture?" Angerman said.

Ruth came over to them. "You should follow their example and make yourselves at home," she said, nodding at the little ones. "Please go shopping and help yourselves to anything you want. Clothes, toys . . . we have everything you need here at the Crossroads. And take your time; it's special extended shopping hours! We don't have to be at the Food Court for a while yet. That's upstairs on the second floor."

Angerman glanced around. He noticed that Teacher was heading over to a store called the Book Nook. Hunter was checking out Mountain Sports, next door. The girl in the khakis had disappeared.

Mommy grabbed Angerman's arm and began leading him across the hall, toward a store called the Gap. "Look at those nice new clothes—we can get nice new clothes for ourselves and the little ones!" she exclaimed.

Angerman stared at the display window of the Gap and stopped in his tracks.

The display window was full of Bad Guys. One, two, three, four, five, *six* Bad Guys. They weren't naked like his Bad Guy but dressed in jeans, skirts, brightly colored shirts and sweaters. None of them had heads.

Brothers and sisters, amen! Bad Guy cried out.

"You go," Angerman ordered Mommy in a gruff voice. "I don't need anything."

"But—" Mommy protested.

"Just go!" He wrenched his arm away from her and turned back toward Santa's workshop, where Action Figure was teaching Puppy and Kitty how to pull the antlers off the reindeer.

Everyone was gathered in the Food Court for the Communal Evening Meal. Men in blue wandered around, lighting giant torches with matches as darkness fell outside. The women, who had prepared the meals in the kitchen of the China Bowl, served everyone at their tables.

Mommy squirmed around in her chair, trying to get used to her new clothes. She had found a pink-and-black plaid skirt at the Gap and a matching pink blouse with pearl buttons at a store called Banana Republic. The material of the blouse itched a bit. But it was so pretty; she would have to learn to live with it. She also had new white socks and black leather shoes that pinched her feet.

The price tags were still on the clothes. The tag on the skirt said $59.00, and the tag on the blouse said $39.00. She didn't want to cut them off. It had been so long since she'd done real shopping in a real store, not just worn the clothes Hunter had hunted for her at dead people's houses. She fingered the price tags, and tried to remember money. Buying stuff instead of just taking it.

"Would you like a cupcake, Sister?"

Mommy glanced up. One of the Crossroads women was standing over her table, holding a plate of cupcakes. The cake part was yellow, and there was brown frosting on top. Mommy couldn't remember the last time she or the other children had eaten cupcakes. *Accept No Substitutes*, said the commandment. "Yes!" she said. "Yes, please, I mean. And thank you!"

Baby and Doll, who were sitting at the table with her, also took cupcakes. Baby and Doll were only three at the time of Fire-us—it was possible that they'd never even *had* cupcakes, or if they had, they sure didn't remember it. Mommy didn't know much about their lives in the Before Time. She hadn't found them until after Fire-us.

Baby took one bite of her cupcake, then another, then another, stuffing it in with greedy delight. Her mouth was soon smeared with chocolate, as was her new red dress from Gap Kids. "Mmm, mmm, good!"

"Mommy, can we have cupcakes *all* the time?" Doll begged with her mouth full. She was wearing the same dress as Baby, in turquoise.

Mommy smiled. "We'll see."

She took a small, tentative bite of her cupcake. She closed her eyes, savoring the taste. It was wonderful, heavenly. Especially after living on dried beef and peanut butter and canned tuna these last five years—whatever was left on the shelves of Winn Dixie and Publix that the rats and other wild animals couldn't get into.

Teacher and Hunter were sitting at the next table, along with Action Figure and Teddy Bear. Teacher's cupcake lay untouched on her plate. She was bent over

The Book, writing like mad with a new orange marker she'd gotten at Office Depot. The boys were devouring their cupcakes and laughing about something. They all had new clothes. They looked so happy. It had been a long time since they could all relax this way.

Angerman was sitting two tables over, with the twins. He was the only one who had refused to go shopping. He was still wearing his dirty old fatigues that were covered with mud from their long boat trip down the river. Bad Guy was on the floor beside him, facedown. Mommy noticed that Angerman had one foot perched on the mannequin's back.

After the cupcakes, the women served more food: spaghetti with tomato sauce and Parmesan cheese, canned peaches, grape juice. Everything was so yummy, not what Mommy was used to at all. Baby and Doll raced through their food, then went over to play with some children who were tossing a ball around in front of Papaya Joe's. There were only a few children at the mall—otherwise it was all Grown-ups.

Ruth Tooten and another woman came and stood over Mommy's table. Ruth beamed at Mommy. "Is your meal okay?"

"It's delicious, thank you," Mommy said.

Ruth sat down in Baby's chair. The other woman sat in Doll's. Mommy noticed the woman staring with curiosity at Doll's dolly, which only had one eye. "We'll have to get her a new one at Toy World," the woman remarked.

"This is Proverbs 22:15," Ruth told Mommy, nodding at the woman.

Mommy cocked her head. "22:15? Like numbers?

Is that your last name?"

"Yes," Ruth replied. "We are named for verses in Holy Scripture."

Mommy couldn't remember her own last name—or her first name, for that matter. None of them were really sure what their old Before Time names were. She had found a book with the name Annie Ginkel in it, in a car on the way out of Lazarus that made her feel strange and fluttery and tearful inside. But she wasn't sure if that meant it had been her family's car, if it meant that it was her book from the Before Time, if it meant her name was Annie Ginkel. Hunter always said he was pretty sure that was his old name, but maybe it wasn't. He was a hunter, so he was called Hunter. That's how they did it.

"I just wanted to tell you, we're all so impressed," Proverbs 22:15 said to Mommy. "You've obviously been an excellent mother to these little ones all these years. Feeding them, clothing them, making sure they stay healthy. And here you are, what? Fifteen, sixteen?"

"Fourteen," Mommy said.

"Only fourteen!" Ruth exclaimed. "That's even more impressive, then. You are an amazing young lady."

Proverbs 22:15 touched Mommy's arm. "I hope you feel like you can breathe easy now, because we're here to help you with the little ones. Isn't that right, Ruth 2:10?"

Mommy smiled and nodded. She glanced down at her plate, at what remained of her spaghetti and peaches and cupcake. She felt all mixed-up about what the women were saying. On the one hand, she was glad that the family was in a safe place now, where there was plentiful food and nice, new clothes and Grown-ups to watch over them.

But on the other hand, did this mean she would stop being a mommy to the little ones? Would they get new mommies? She had spent the last five years being a mommy to Baby and Doll and Action Figure and Teddy Bear—and more recently, to Puppy and Kitty. Would they all stop calling her Mommy? What would they start calling her? She hoped they didn't start calling her something with numbers in it.

Proverbs 22:15's voice cut into her thoughts. "Those two little ones over there," she said, gesturing to Puppy and Kitty. "They're twins, aren't they? So adorable! How old are they?"

"We figure they're about five," Mommy explained. "They've only been with us for a short while. We kept seeing them running around Lazarus—that's where we were living. They were so skinny and starving looking, but they were too scared to let us come near. We finally had to catch them with bait and a trap Hunter and Action Figure made, out of a box. We figure whoever was taking care of them . . . well, you know, *died*."

Mommy said the word *died* in a whisper. She felt shivery all of a sudden, even though it was very warm in the Food Court. She hated thinking of Puppy and Kitty losing someone they loved. They were so young, just babies—too young to go through something like that.

Of course, they had *all* been too young to go through something like that.

"They're five years old, you say?" Ruth 2:10 said to Mommy.

"Yup," Mommy replied. Then she remembered Manners. "I mean, yes, ma'am."

Ruth 2:10 and Proverbs 22:15 exchanged a glance.

* * *

At the next table, Hunter speared the last of his spaghetti into his mouth. The rations were really good here, and he was glad to be under cover and out of the elements. Still, he felt a grumble of dissatisfaction inside. The fact was, he didn't feel 100 percent welcome.

He squinted over at Mommy, who was chatting with Ruth 2:10 and another woman. His magic sunglasses—the ones that made him see so well—were useless this time of day when it was too dark. The women were obviously making Mommy feel at home, making her feel like one of them. And Ruth 2:10 had spent a lot of time with Teacher before dinner, talking to her about The Book.

But Hunter hadn't received the same sort of welcome from the men of the Crossroads Mall. These guys hadn't said a word to him since he and the others arrived this afternoon. Didn't they realize he was the man of their small family? Didn't they realize he was *important*?

He glanced at Teacher, who was scribbling in The Book. Action Figure and Teddy Bear had gone off to play. "What're you writing?" he asked Teacher.

"I'm recording the events of this afternoon," Teacher replied without looking up.

"Excuse me."

The girl was standing there. Hunter had noticed her earlier. Her eyes went right to Teacher and didn't seem to take him in at all. "Excuse me, hi, I didn't get to introduce myself before. I'm Corinthians 1:19," she said.

Teacher stared at her and didn't say anything. "I'm Hunter and this is Teacher," Hunter said, trying to fill the awkward silence. "Corinthians 1:19. You have one of those names with numbers, too?"

Corinthians 1:19 sat down in the chair Action Figure had left. She leaned forward and whispered, "Yeah, we all do. But you can call me Cory, as long as you don't do it in front of the others."

"Do your First Mommy and First Daddy live at Crossroads Mall, too?" Hunter asked her. It occurred to him that if he became friends with Cory, he might become friends with her father, too. That would give him an in with the men.

Cory started. "If you mean my mother and father—they're dead. They died before the Great Flame. I had an older sister who lived here for a while, but she, um . . . she's gone. She disappeared."

Hunter was about to ask Cory what that meant, *disappeared*, but she didn't give him a chance. "What's that?" she asked Teacher, pointing to The Book.

Teacher's eyes widened. She slammed The Book shut. "It's . . . kind of hard to explain."

"Is it what they used to call *book* in the olden times?" Cory asked.

"Don't you have books here?" Teacher asked her. "I went to a store called the Book Nook earlier. All the shelves were empty."

"Someone burned all the books in the mall," Cory whispered. She reached across the table and touched The Book. "Please, won't you let me see it?" she pleaded.

Teacher flinched and pulled The Book away from Cory. "No! No one can see The Book but me. It's sacred!"

There was a loud scraping of chairs all around. Everyone was getting up from the tables.

Ruth 2:10 got up from her table and came over to Hunter, Teacher, and Cory. "It's time for the meeting, Corinthians 1:19," Ruth 2:10 announced.

Cory dabbed at her eyes and rose to her feet. "Of course. Thank you, Sister."

"You're invited to come as well," Ruth 2:10 said to Teacher and Hunter. Her gaze lingered on The Book, which Teacher was hugging against her chest. "I think you'll find it very enlightening."

"Will the men be there?" Hunter asked Ruth 2:10.

"Of course. We all attend."

Hunter grinned and got up from his chair. Maybe *this* would be his chance to get in with the guys, he thought. Without waiting for Ruth 2:10 and Cory and Teacher, he raced ahead to where a group of blue-clad men were talking in quiet voices and moving as one in the direction of the Cine-Theater 6.

Chapter Three

Angerman set down his water glass and pressed his index finger into the remaining cupcake crumbs scattered on the table in front of him, sticking them to his skin. As he raised his finger to his mouth, he realized that everyone was streaming out of the Food Court, heading in the same direction. He sucked the crumbs off his finger, watching the Grown-ups, and then glanced around to see what the other kids in his family were going to do.

This meeting will now come to order, Bad Guy whispered. *You're probably all wondering why I called you here today. I have good news and bad news. Which would you like to hear first?*

Angerman pressed down on the mannequin's neck a little harder with his foot.

"I guess we're supposed to go," Mommy said with a look over to the next table at Teacher.

They pushed their chairs back, and hushed the grumbles from the little ones who had just run back to the table, begging for more cupcakes. Angerman tapped Puppy and Kitty on the tops of their heads. "Come on, you two, too," he said and reached down to swing Bad Guy in his knapsack onto his back.

They reached out to take his hands, and they followed Mommy and the others through the mall, past the shadowy stores, beneath the holiday tinsel stars that dangled from the high ceiling and moved in an intangible current of air. The Grown-ups were filing in through the doors of Cine-Theater 6 in silence, and it was clear that the few children that lived at the Crossroads were trying hard to be respectful. Hunter was waiting for his family at the door, obviously impatient for them to catch up so they could join the group. Angerman gripped Puppy's and Kitty's hands a little tighter as they passed the movie theater's big concession stand.

For an extra thirty cents you can get a supersize with unlimited refills.

In the theater, the men and women sorted themselves out—men sitting on the left, and women on the right, while the Crossroads kids took seats in the front row. Flaring torches duct-taped to brackets on the walls gave the place a shifting light. The ceiling was blackened with smoke and soot, and the air was hot and harsh smelling.

"Amazing this place doesn't catch on fire," Angerman said under his breath.

"Let's sit in here," Hunter whispered, standing to one side and ushering Teacher and Mommy and the others into a middle row near the back. Action Figure slammed the seats down, grinning as they snapped back up, but the hush of the room seemed to affect him and he took a seat without making any more noise. Angerman took a moment to pick up Puppy and Kitty and sit them each in a plush red seat, and while his back was turned to the screen, Bad Guy spoke in a loud, commanding voice.

"Brothers and Sisters!"

"Brothers and Sisters," replied the Grown-ups in response.

Shocked, Angerman grappled the knapsack off his back to give the mannequin a hard slap in the face, but as he turned he realized that it was someone else who had spoken. A tall man in blue stood on a raised platform at the front of the theater, arms spread wide. It hadn't been Bad Guy who'd spoken—it was this man, but the voice and the intonation were similar. A slight shudder of fear raced up Angerman's spine. He clutched the knapsack and sat down, trying not to let his worry show.

"It's a great day," the man said, looking out over the congregation. The torchlight threw deep shadows into his face, and made his smile goblinlike.

Teacher tipped her head toward Angerman. "Hey, I just noticed something," she hissed. "See how they're dressed? I didn't realize it before."

Angerman looked from side to side. All the men were in some combination of blue clothes—denim jeans or blue suits or workshirts. And all the women were wearing white or off-white—dresses, tunic-like shirts, wide-legged pants, or white leggings. It hadn't been so obvious before, with everyone mingled together, especially as it seemed the kids wore any old combination of clothes and colors they wanted.

"It's a little weird, don't you think?" Teacher continued.

Hunter jabbed at her with his elbow and put a finger to his lips. Angerman and Teacher slumped a little lower in their seats.

"It's a great day, indeed," the man repeated. "For today we have had a glimpse of something wonderful, something that may be our future, our New Savior—"

The New Jerusalem! Praise the Lord!

"And yet even in the midst of our rejoicing, we must not let ourselves be fooled and deceived into giving up our quest, for the Devil comes in many disguises—"

Amen, brothers and sisters!

"And it is often when we think our redemption is at hand that we see the claws of the Beast reaching out to steal our souls."

Praise the Lord!

Angerman wiped one shaking hand across his mouth. He couldn't tell who it was crying out—Bad Guy or some of the Grown-ups in the audience. His other hand was pressed down so hard across Bad Guy's plastic mouth that it should have been impossible for him to speak, but could he anyway? Or was he maybe making other people speak? There was no telling what Bad Guy might do—he was capable of anything. Angerman kept his head down and cast furtive glances from side to side. Teacher was looking at the preacher, or leader or whoever the speaker was, and her expression was puzzled and slightly disgusted—but she didn't seem to have heard anything from Bad Guy. She wasn't looking at him or anything. Still, Angerman's pulse raced with fear, and his face felt hot.

"Let us remember our dear sister, Corinthians 1:19, who will soon take her part in this most holy quest," the speaker went on. "As she prepares for the blessing that is Union, our hearts are with her."

"That's that blond girl."

Angerman stared at Teacher. He could hear his own

heart thudding in his ears. "Did you say something?" he whispered.

"I said that's that blond girl he's talking about," she muttered, jutting her chin toward a girl seated three rows ahead of them in the middle section. "You know, this reminds me of Church. Did you ever go to Church?"

Did we ever go to church! Merciful heavens! Sunday morning, ten o'clock, Onward Christian Soldiers! And let's remember to say a prayer in our hearts for those who aren't with us today, and for the afflicted, the poor, those who have fallen away from the path of the righteous AND PRAISE THE LORD and those who haven't yet found the light of—

Angerman knew the man was talking, could see the man's lips moving, but Bad Guy was yammering so loudly that he couldn't hear. There was nothing he could do to stop the flow of words and exclamations and laughter tumbling out of Bad Guy's mouth. Angerman looked around at the faces staring in rapt attention at the speaker. The light of the torches bending first one way and then another made them look as if they were all being consumed by a bonfire. He squeezed his eyes shut and wrapped his hands around Bad Guy's throat. He tried to think of normal things, but nothing was normal, nothing had been normal for five years, and all that came to him was the sign painted on the highway that had drawn him to Lazarus: WE'RE STILL HERE. A sob rose in his throat. He was choking.

"Come on—it's over," Teacher was saying.

Angerman opened his eyes. People were standing up and shaking hands with each other, giving the Kiss of

Peace, smiling and chatting. Children were running up the aisles and pulling toys out of their pockets. Angerman tightened his grip on Bad Guy's throat and drew the mannequin in close to him, as if it were a grenade about to go off that he had to protect everyone from.

He turned pleading eyes to Teacher, who was standing up, waiting for him. Her expression changed to alarm. "What is it?" she asked.

"Get me out of here," Angerman begged through gritted teeth. "Get. Me. Out. Of. Here."

Teacher took Teddy Bear's hand and sidestepped out of the row. She looked back over her shoulder to see how Angerman was doing. He was sidling out of the row, too, holding Bad Guy out in front of him like a deadly snake. Two women stepped into the row from the opposite end, reaching down to pick up Puppy and Kitty. Teacher's heart leaped.

"What are you doing?" she called out, and even as she spoke, reaching the end of the row, Ruth 2:10 knelt down in front of Teddy Bear and put her arms around him.

"We're going to take these youngsters to our children's dormitory," Ruth 2:10 said with a reassuring smile. "It's the quietest part of the Crossroads, and we'll give them baths and new clean pjs." She picked Teddy Bear up, and he gave her a shy, sleepy smile. "By the Flame, you're a big boy, aren't you?"

Mommy stood stock-still in the aisle while women surrounded Baby and Doll and Action Figure. Her forehead was creased, and she had an uncertain smile on her face. She looked sick or embarrassed. "Oh, well, they always sleep with us," she faltered. "It's really okay, you don't have to—"

"Now listen," Ruth 2:10 said, hitching Teddy Bear a little higher on her hip. "You kids have had this weight on your shoulders for years, and you need to give yourselves a break. Now, it's all decided! No argument."

Teacher came to Mommy's side and held her hand. Together, they watched the women walk up the aisle, bearing all the little ones away and out of the theater. Teacher could feel sweat on Mommy's palm. "It'll be okay," she said, as much for her own benefit as for Mommy's.

"I'll, um, I can show you where you'll sleep."

They turned around. Cory was behind them, casting puzzled glances at Angerman, who stood muttering under his breath at Bad Guy and making horrible faces. She managed a weak smile. "Come on—it's this way."

Nobody spoke as Cory led the way up to the second level. Angerman was working himself up into some kind of frenzy attack, and Teacher and the others didn't want to have to explain him to the strange girl. They did not meet one another's eyes. Teacher kept a tight grip on The Book, itching to have some privacy so she could write down what the guy had said during the meeting. It had been so strange. She couldn't remember if Grown-ups used to be this way. It was so hard to remember. Her memories of Going to Church were very hazy, so she couldn't say what it was about this meeting that reminded her of it. Once they were all alone, they'd be able to discuss it. But not in front of Cory. The girl made Teacher nervous.

The place set aside for them to sleep in was a store on the second level called Futon-a-Rama. Thick cotton mattresses had been made up with sheets and pillows, and a battery-powered camping lantern made a pool of ghostly blue light among them. Cory picked up a smaller flashlight and switched it on, pointing its beam toward the back of the store.

"I think they put some pajamas and things for you back there where you can change," she said in a low voice. She made no move to leave but stood there fiddling with the flashlight.

"Umm, thanks," Teacher said. She cast a look at Hunter. He shrugged.

"You'll be sorry," Angerman growled, bumping into things as he wandered around the store. "Oh-ho, boy, will you be sorry."

Teacher saw Cory look at Angerman and then away, trying not to stare.

"Everyone comfortable?" Ruth 2:10 walked into Futon-a-Rama, her white tunic billowing around her as she moved. She put a hand on Mommy's shoulder in a loving gesture. "You deserve a night of carefree dreams. Wasn't Deuteronomy 29:28 inspiring tonight?"

"Are the children okay?" Mommy asked.

Ruth 2:10 clucked her tongue. "Now, now. They're fine. Don't worry about them."

From the corner of her eye, Teacher noticed that Angerman had put Bad Guy facedown on a futon and was trying to smother him. His eyes were wide and staring. She turned to Ruth 2:10 and spoke in a false, bright tone, taking a step toward the door. "Ruth, do you think tomorrow maybe you or someone else could explain to us everything that happened? You know, back then? I've tried to keep a record of everything, but there's a lot we can't remember or that we didn't understand."

Ruth 2:10 followed her toward the door, and Cory fell into step with them.

"You must have quite a lot written in that book of yours," Ruth 2:10 said. "But why dwell on the past?"

Cory broke in. "Do you write it all down? Everything?"

Teacher stiffened and drew away from Cory. She couldn't bring herself to answer.

"Maybe I could tell you some things that happened," Cory continued.

"Corinthians 1:19, you've got a big day ahead of you tomorrow," Ruth 2:10 said in a warning tone. She put her arm around Cory's shoulders. "Another fitting, and I think more lessons—isn't that right? So you won't have time for anything else."

As Ruth 2:10 walked Cory out the door, Teacher held The Book behind her back. Cory cast one look over her shoulder at Teacher and the others, and then disappeared into the darkness.

"Whew!" Teacher let out a sigh and walked back toward the pool of lantern light. "That girl is freaky."

"You ain't seen nothing yet," Angerman spoke up. He sat up on the bed, squaring his shoulders and putting on his fake newsman smile, his anchorman smile. He held up his old picture frame. "Earlier today, ten children ranging in age from five to fifteen were found in a lifeboat, after completing a journey of several thousand miles through mosquito-infested swamps.

Repeated attacks by Antichrists had left them weak and frightened—woops! Ex*cuse* me that's alligators! Funny, even the alphabet seems to have been affected by this Apocalypse, can't trust anything or ANYONE!!!! News from the Centers for Disease Control sent Wall Street into a tailspin, but here at the Crossroads there's something for everyone! Mom, Dad, Sis, and Junior! The elect—the select—the selection is great! And don't forget to pick up some Salvation for your family because any day now we're all going to—"

"Stop it!" Mommy cried out. She ran to Angerman and shook him by the shoulders. "Please don't do this!"

"—all going to die, that's right. But not here at the Crossroads! Join us! You'll be Saved. The savings can't be beat!"

Hunter threw a desperate look out toward the interior of the mall. "Shut up—someone will hear you!" he warned. "Do you want us to get kicked out?"

The life seemed to go out of Angerman. He slumped, and his head drooped forward over his chest. Teacher stepped closer to him. She could hear him whispering something as he pulled the legless mannequin onto his lap.

"Why did you do it?" he asked. He began to cry.

Teacher sank to the floor beside him and rested The Book on the futon where the light fell on it. She opened to a fresh page, dug her new pen out of her pocket, and wrote down Angerman's last question.

Why did you do it? She underlined it, and looked up at Angerman's shadowed face. "Do what? Are you asking *him*? Is Bad Guy—is he *answering* you now?"

Angerman looked up and swiped his tears away with a rough gesture. "No. That's the problem. He won't say."

* * *

Mommy reached out in her sleep for Baby and Doll, but their warm small bodies weren't there. She was instantly awake, heart pounding. It took her a moment to remind herself that all was well, and with a small sigh, she rolled onto one shoulder and opened her eyes. The lantern was still glowing. Teacher was sitting on the floor, The Book on her lap. On two other futons, the boys were sound asleep.

"Are you reading?" Mommy asked, her voice soft.

Teacher looked over and shook her head without speaking. Then she set The Book down and stepped over the lantern to climb into bed beside Mommy. Mommy pulled the sheet up over Teacher's thin arms, and they put their heads together on the pillow. Above them, the ceiling was lost in darkness. The world was totally silent but for the sound of the boys' breathing.

"Well," Mommy said after a while. "What do you think?"

"I don't know what to think," Teacher replied. "I keep trying to remember if Grown-ups were always like this."

Mommy frowned. Her babies weren't there. The grief threatened to rush back. "Like what?"

"Don't they seem—" Teacher shook her head, and the pillowcase made a soft shushing sound under her cheek. "I don't know . . ."

"I wish they didn't take the kids away from us," Mommy whispered. "It makes me feel all empty, like a cup that spilled."

"But they said they'd give the kids baths and pjs and they can be with the other kids."

"I know, but . . . I guess I should be glad. I'm being stupid, I guess. We've wanted to find Grown-ups and now we have. They've got food and a good place to live. And it's safe . . ."

"Not for Angerman."

Mommy raised herself up on her elbow, looked down at Teacher and then over at Angerman's sleeping form. Bad Guy was lying next to Angerman, his painted plastic eyes staring at the ceiling. "Yeah, is he getting worse since we got here? It's hard to tell."

"Since Jacksonville this morning," Teacher replied. She turned her head to look over at Angerman, too. "There was a picture painted on a bridge—did you see it? He looked at it and I thought for a moment he was going to scream. Like he'd just seen the most terrible thing on earth."

Mommy nodded. A gray horse. A gray horse painted on the side of a metal bridge they went under in their boat. "He pretended nothing was wrong, but I think he was listening to Bad Guy. They talk to each other, have you noticed?"

"Yeah." Teacher shivered a little bit, then pulled the sheet closer under her chin. "I'm worried about him." Her mouth stretched in a huge yawn.

"So much happened today," Mommy said, settling back down again. She yawned, too, and suddenly realized how exhausted she was. It had to be because she was so weary that her heart was full of uncertainty and misgiving. Things would be clearer in the morning, and she'd be happy that they had come to the Crossroads. It was just tiredness and the weeks of fear that was wearing her down, now. It would all be much better in the morning. She opened her mouth to say something else, but saw that Teacher was asleep. Mommy snuggled closer to her friend, and let the darkness come.

Chapter Four

Early morning sun poured through the skylights and lit up the mirrored walls, the display windows, the big silver letters that spelled THIS WAY TO ENTRANCE EAST. The brightness was dazzling, almost blinding, so that Hunter had to shield his eyes as he walked through the atrium. He could go back to the Futon-a-Rama and get his sunglasses, but he didn't feel like it. What he really felt like doing was getting to the Food Court as soon as possible, so he could enjoy the experience of being fed by Grown-ups again, of eating as much as he pleased. It had been five whole years since he had done that.

He had even slept in a bit this morning. Sleeping in, what a treat! Or what a Bonus, which is what Mommy called candy bars and gum and other special things he used to find for the family. Mommy, Angerman, and Teacher had all woken up before him and left to go to the Food Court, to meet up with the little ones. On her way out the door Mommy had called Hunter's name, but he had just mumbled something incoherent in response and nestled deeper, deeper under the pillowy-soft Sweet-Dreams Extra-Deluxe comforter, 100% goose-down filled, $99.95, Warning Contents May Be Flammable.

That was another Bonus. Because the bed had been so comfortable, because they were finally in a safe place, he had slept through the night without waking. It had been a long time since he had been able to sleep in peace, without being roused by the screams of panthers or worrying about Action Figure sneaking out of the house with his bow and arrow—*bone arra*, he always called them.

On the other hand, there had been dreams. And maybe not such sweet ones, either. The meeting at the Cine-Theater, had that been a dream? Images danced through Hunter's head: the enormous dark theater, the flames from the torches curling and spitting in the air, the rows and rows of identical plush seats, men on one side and women on the other. The children had sat in the middle, still and silent as statues. And the older guy— Dieter Astronomy or something—had stood with his back to the huge blank movie screen, preaching to the Crossroads families and Hunter's family about fire . . . about the New Savior . . . about *reeeeeeedemption and hope Brothers and Sisters amen!*

"Good morning, Brother."

Hunter stopped and turned around. A couple of Grown-ups, both men, were coming out of the Men's Wearhouse. They were carrying a bunch of packages wrapped in dark blue plastic. The taller one raised his right hand, palm facing Hunter, and held it there.

Hunter tried to say something, but his mouth felt dry like cotton. This was the first time any of the Crossroads men had spoken to him.

"M-morning," he finally managed to stammer.

The tall man lowered his hand. "Why don't you join us after the Communal Morning Meal, Brother," he said in a friendly enough voice. "All the older Brothers tend to the horses out at the loading dock around the corner from Entrance East. It's part of the Daily Strengthening."

"Yes, I'll be there," he said, barely able to contain his excitement.

And then a thought occurred to him. "What about Angerman? Should I ask him to come to the, um, Daily Strengthening, too?"

The two men exchanged a glance. "That will not be necessary," the tall man said.

"You are more like us than he is," the other man explained.

Hunter wasn't sure what that was supposed to mean, exactly. But he felt himself pushing his shoulders back, standing a little straighter as he said, "Well, I guess that might be true."

"By the Flame."

"By the Flame."

By the . . . what? Hunter wanted to ask. But before he had a chance, the two men turned on their heels and walked into the bright light of the atrium, in the direction of the Food Court.

Hunter followed, not saying any more, just grinning from ear to ear. Things were definitely looking up. And it was probably just as well about Angerman. The guy seemed to be getting crazier all the time, anyway—just look at the way he was acting last night! Teacher kept insisting that according to The Book, Angerman was meant to come to Lazarus, was meant to be with them. But Hunter had never quite believed that. Not that he was one to contradict The Book, which was sacred, but so far Angerman had mostly been nothing but trouble and bad news.

At the Food Court, Hunter found his family having

breakfast at two adjoining tables: Mommy, Baby, Doll, and Teacher at one, and Teddy Bear, Action Figure, and Angerman at the other. No sign of Puppy and Kitty. The Crossroads Grown-ups and their children were sitting at the other tables, eating and talking in quiet voices. As with dinner last night—no, not dinner, Hunter corrected himself, the Communal Evening Meal—various women were serving the food. This morning it was Ruth 2:10 and that Proverbs-something and Corinthy with the long blond braid. Cory.

Hunter pulled up a chair next to his brother and sat down. "Hey, what're you eatin'?" he asked, ruffling Action Figure's white-blond hair. He realized with a start that the boy's hair was clean. Clean! His face and fingernails were clean, too, probably for the first time in years. It occurred to Hunter that the women must have managed to give him a bath last night, which was not an insignificant feat.

Action Figure picked up a wedge of toast with his fingers and dangled it in the air as though it were a small, dead animal. "Breadenbudder," he announced with glee. He stuffed it in his mouth and chewed, letting melted butter run down his chin.

"So much for the clean face," Hunter said with a laugh. "Mommy will have a fit when she sees you forgot Manners again."

On the other hand, when was the last time the family had tasted butter? The Crossroads people must have their own cow, as well as a . . . what was it called in the Before Time? A butter turn—something like that.

Ruth 2:10 came over to their table and set a plate

in front of Hunter. "Good morning, Brother. Won't you have some toast and eggs?"

"Wow, you've got real chickens?" Hunter couldn't remember the last time he had tasted eggs. Although the smell of them, fried like that, touched some place in his brain, some distant Sunday-morning memory. "Thank you," he said, picking up his fork.

"Miss Ruth," Mommy called out from the other table. "Excuse me, but we were wondering about the twins, Puppy and Kitty. . . ." There was an edge in her voice that made Hunter put his fork down and turn around.

Ruth 2:10 gave Mommy a serene smile. "They're still asleep, the sweet little babies. They were so tired after your long river journey."

"Oh," Mommy said. "Well, then . . . could I see them for just a minute? I'm their Mommy—I need to be with them when they wake up."

Ruth 2:10 continued to smile. "That's not a good idea, dear. Here, would you like more toast?"

Proverbs-something came over to Ruth 2:10's side, holding a pitcher of milk. She beamed at Mommy. "You are *such* a good mother, always thinking of your babies," she murmured.

"It's remarkable, considering how young she is and all," Ruth 2:10 agreed.

"More milk, more milk!" Baby began to clamor, banging her cup on the table.

"Hush, that's no way to ask," Mommy whispered to her. "Milk, *please*. Do Manners."

Proverbs poured Baby more milk, then she and Ruth 2:10 drifted away to serve the other tables. Hunter leaned over to Mommy and whispered, "Don't worry about the wild ones, they'll be fine. These Grown-ups know how to take care of children. Look, they gave Action a bath!"

"I suppose so," Mommy said, not sounding totally sure.

"Don't worry," he repeated. Without waiting for her to reply, he turned back to his plate and began ploughing through his food. It was delicious, and he would have enjoyed it more if he weren't so eager to be finished and on his way to the loading dock.

Out of the corner of his eye, he saw some of the other men putting their forks down and scooting back their chairs. Hunter put his fork down and scooted his chair back, too. *Don't Delay!*

"Where're you goin'?" Action Figure demanded.

"To the loading dock. Some of the men asked me to join them," Hunter explained.

The boy's green eyes gleamed. "Goin' with you!" he cried out.

Hunter shook his head. "No, you're not. This is for the big guys only."

"Goin' with you!" Action Figure insisted.

"No . . . you're . . . *not*." Hunter got up. "Teddy, you enjoying your eggs?"

Teddy Bear nodded. "Yessir, enjoying these eggs."

"That's my man."

Hunter walked away, not wanting to argue with his brother anymore. Action Figure could hang out with Teddy Bear. The two boys could explore the mall together or something.

Hunter headed into the atrium. There was a store

that he hadn't noticed yesterday, next to the Holiday Shoppe. He stopped and squinted at the sign: Myoptica. The display window was full of glasses, nothing but glasses, perched on cubes of shiny, clear plastic.

"Is this my lucky day or what," Hunter said out loud.

When he walked out of Myoptica five minutes later, he was wearing a pair of silver-rimmed glasses. He'd found them on the counter, in a black case with a handwritten label attached to it: READY FOR PICKUP, CALL TIFFANY SNYDER OR HER MOTHER 555-3129. The lenses were clear, not like the dark ones in his sunglasses. And now he could see everything: the tiniest merchandise in the display windows; the small THANK YOU FOR NOT SMOKING! signs; the blue-clad men in the distance, rushing out of Entrance East.

Hunter smiled, adjusted his new glasses, and hurried off in the direction of the men.

"By the Flame, aren't these little girls pretty in their bridesmaid's dresses!"

"They'll make wonderful Brides someday, won't they?"

Mommy glanced up from her chair, where one of the Crossroads women, Micah 2:9, was giving her something called a manna-cure. Baby and Doll were running around Danielle's Bridal Shoppe dressed in lacy pink dresses that were several sizes too big for them. Baby had a matching pink bow in her hair. Doll was wearing a white veil that dragged on the ground behind her.

"We're princesses, we're princesses!" Baby squealed.

"Just like Coreetheenee!" Doll added.

The little girls pranced to the center of the room, where that Cory girl was standing up on a carpeted stool, above everyone. She was wearing a fancy white dress that went down to her bare feet. It looked tight, too tight, like how could you breathe in that? Two of the Crossroads women, Proverbs 3:21 and Psalm 12, were circling Cory with pins and scissors.

Mommy realized with a flicker of surprise that it was a wedding dress. She tried hard to remember what that meant. Women wore wedding dresses in the Before Time when they were ready to have husbands, when they wanted to become First Mommies. Mommy felt her right hand being grabbed by Micah 2:9.

"There, you're going to look beautiful, too, Mommy," the woman cooed, brushing Mommy's nails with pale pink paint. "Perhaps you'll be lucky enough to be a Bride yourself someday!"

"What a lovely thought, Micah 2:9," Psalm 12 agreed. "Perhaps someday soon!"

Mommy glanced down at her nails. The pink on them was sparkly and pretty. Mommy couldn't help but smile. This was nice, this manna-cure. It had been a long time since she had felt so pretty, so taken care of. She had been taking care of everyone else—no one ever looked after her like this.

It was nice to see her little girls so happy, too. Now, if only she could see Puppy and Kitty . . .

"It'll be your turn next, Teacher," Micah 2:9 called out. Teacher was sitting cross-legged on the floor, half hidden by a rack of white dresses that were squeezed and bunched together on hangers. Mommy could see that she was writing something in The Book.

Teacher shook her head without looking up. "No, thanks."

"Oh, come on, Teacher," chided Proverbs 3:21. "We all know you're a wise old owl with your little book, but you can enjoy being a girl, too! Isn't that right, Mommy?"

Cory made a sudden jerking motion, making Proverbs 3:21 spill all her pins. "Corinthians 1:19, look what you made me do! By the Flame, what is the matter with you today?"

Mommy stared at Cory in surprise. Cory's face had become as colorless as her dress.

"If you don't stand still, we're never going to have your dress ready in time," Psalm 12 scolded her.

"Are you . . . are you getting married?" Mommy asked Cory in a hesitant voice. "Who are you getting married to?" She knew she was being nosy, but her curiosity had gotten the best of her. Cory didn't look to be any older than she was. If Cory was getting married, did that mean it was time for Mommy to be getting married, too?

"Well—" Cory began. But Micah 2:9 interrupted her, exclaiming, "Corinthians 1:19 has been chosen for a very special honor!"

"Honor? What honor?" Mommy asked.

"By the Flame, someone help me with these pins!" Proverbs 3:21 cried out. "Those little girls are going to step on them. Corinthians 1:19, you really need to learn to be more still."

The three women fell to their knees and began gathering pins. Mommy glanced up at Cory, and their eyes met. Something . . . something in Cory's expression told her that she wasn't exactly happy about having been chosen—whatever *chosen* meant.

It was almost time for the Communal Midday Meal. Behind the rack of wedding dresses, Cory buttoned up her plaid shirt with stiff, fumbling fingers and yanked on her khaki pants. Through the mist of gauzy white, she could just make out the others in the room. Those little girls were sprawled out on the floor, picking through a pile of ribbons and sashes. The one named Mommy was sitting next to them, blowing on her nails and laughing.

Psalm 12 and Proverbs 3:21 were over by the cash register hanging up Cory's dress, trying to tame the rustling fabric into a plastic bag. They smiled and cooed as they ran their hands over the chest part, where rows of tiny seed pearls formed an elaborate X.

"Corinthians 1:19 is going to make us all so proud!" Psalm 12 exclaimed.

"By the Flame!"

Cory scowled to herself and parted the bunched-up dresses a little, to see better. Teacher was in the chair that Mommy had occupied before. Micah 2:9 had finally convinced Teacher to have a manicure, and was painting her nails with bright purple nail polish.

Cory's heart raced at the sight of Teacher. It was so clear to her now, Teacher was the owl from her Visioning! And Teacher's book, that strange, thick book, must be the owl's book. Once Cory got hold of it, she would be able to see her future. Teacher and her book held the clues to Cory's true path.

For her path surely couldn't be that awful wedding

dress marked with an X.

Cory started to snake through the back of the wedding dress rack. She would head over to the loading dock. The men wouldn't be finished with their Daily Strengthening yet, and she sometimes liked to hide behind the Dumpster and watch them working on the horses.

But before she could slip out, her foot hit something, hard. Stifling a curse, she glanced down. There was a lump of stray white fabric bunched up on the floor.

She bent down and peeled the fabric away. Her breath caught in her throat. It was Teacher's book!

She peered through a gap in the wedding dress rack. Micah 2:9 was still working on Teacher's nails, which meant that Teacher would be stuck in her chair for a while. Everyone else was occupied, too.

It was her chance. She picked up the book—it was heavy, so heavy—and stepped out from behind the rack, into the light. She turned her back to the others and began turning the thick, crusty pages as quietly as possible.

Almost immediately, Cory's head began to pound. There were pictures with letters scribbled over them, but she couldn't figure out what the letters meant. *C-O-M-E B-A-C-K* was written over a picture of a woman. She sounded out the letters in a whisper, but they made no sense. *W-E N-E-E-D A-N-S-W-E-R-S* was written over a picture of a big white house. Again, Cory sounded out the letters, but again, they made no sense.

She continued turning pages, and more pages, trying to find an item that might be related to her Visioning. But it was all nonsense and mystery words and darkness.

Biting back a cry of frustration, she started to close the book.

But something made her stop. She glanced down at the place where the book lay open in her hands.

There were six letters on a page, mixed in with a bunch of other letters:

INGRID

"No!" Cory whispered.

"'Puppy says Ingrid wants more lemonade.' Isn't that interesting?"

Cory whirled around. Psalm 12 was standing behind her, reading the book over her shoulder. Psalm 12 was smiling, but her eyes were blazing at her, like fire.

"What do you suppose that means, Corinthians 1:19?"

Cory gritted her teeth and hugged the book to her chest. But just then Teacher came leaping across the room and tore the book out of her hands. Purple nail polish smeared across the cover. "Give that back! What are you doing with that—give that back!" Teacher cried out.

"You don't understand!" Cory began. She glanced from Teacher to Psalm 12 to the others in the room, who were all staring at her as if she were some sort of wild animal. Without saying another word, she ran out of Danielle's Bridal Shoppe.

She ran and ran through the atrium and down a side hallway, not noticing the curious looks from the older Keepers who were walking around. She didn't even notice the sunlight that was burning through the skylights and nearly blinding her.

Because in her mind, it was the middle of the night, three years ago. Total darkness, Ingrid's breath warm on her face, the two little ones sleeping in her arms. *Cory, honey, I have to go. I'm sorry.*

Cory continued to run, although she knew the hallway would dead-end at the pet shop soon. She swiped at the hot tears that were stinging her eyes and thought, *Ingrid, why didn't you take me with you?*

Chapter Five

The plate glass display window of Bigelow's Housewares was set up with a holiday-dressed dinner table. Laid out upon the holly-printed cloth were four settings complete with fancy dishes, wineglasses, napkins folded into complicated crown shapes, seven pieces of cutlery, and a separate tiny dish of salt at each place. In the center, candlesticks with red twisty candles stood among fake fruit that glittered with some kind of shiny crystal coating—pears and grapes and some other fruits Angerman couldn't quite remember the names for. Staring closely, Angerman could make out the layer of dust collected in the spirals of the candles and in the bowls of the wineglasses. One glass had a dead fly in it. Five years of seaside air had turned the silver forks and knives black. His own reflection in the window made it appear as if he were sitting at the table, with the face of Bad Guy peeking over his shoulder like a waiter asking if he wanted more wine.

I always love state dinners, so festive, so fun! And I can state absolutely that it's time to have that silver polished!

Angerman turned away from the store window in disgust, letting his backpack swing so that Bad Guy's head cracked against the glass.

Owww! Watch out!

"Watch out yourself," Angerman growled. He kept

his head down as he slouched past three women on their way to the east end of the mall. He heard them whisper among themselves as he went by. So what if they thought he was talking to himself? For that matter, so what if they knew he was talking to the mutilated mannequin on his back? Their opinion of him was the least of his concerns.

Without any thought to where he was going, he turned down a corridor, concentrating all his attention on keeping Bad Guy from mouthing off. He walked staring at the tiled floor. He tried counting off tiles by twos, then by threes, then by squares of three or nine. After a while he came to a standstill, determined to count the number of tiles across the corridor so that he could calculate the number in the whole mall. The effort of remembering how to do the math in his head kept Bad Guy quiet.

A sunken garden of dead shrubbery surrounding a dried-out fountain blocked the middle of the hall. Angerman walked around it, keeping count. Then: two small feet in sneakers.

Angerman looked up. Teddy Bear was trying to flatten himself against the end of a bench. He was nearly crawling into the withered plants. In his hand were several pennies scraped up from the bottom of the fountain.

"Teddy, my man," Angerman said. "What're you doing?"

"It's a commandment," Teddy Bear said, his eyes huge. "*Stop Throwing Money Down the Drain!*"

"Right." Angerman nodded. "So what're you hiding for?"

"Nothing," Teddy Bear whispered. "I wasn't looking."

Angerman pictured himself as he appeared to the timid boy, stalking slowly down the corridor pointing at tiles, muttering to himself. He tried to smile, to look Real Normal.

"Bet you're wondering what I'm doing, huh? Just counting. Practicing my times tables."

Teddy Bear's expression brightened. "Like for School? With Teacher?"

"That's right. Just like School," Angerman reassured him.

"I don't think they do School here," Teddy Bear said. He eased himself out from between the bench and the dried brown branches of the fig trees.

Angerman hitched his thumbs into his belt loops. "Nope. No School. Vacation every day."

Teddy Bear began sucking his thumb, but then yanked it out of his mouth, looking sheepish.

Angerman glanced around. He'd either have to get back to counting or find a livelier distraction than meek Teddy Bear. "So where's Action? Aren't you guys together?"

"Umm . . . he . . ." Teddy Bear looked around, and he began to raise his thumb to his mouth again until he remembered not to. "I think he went to find Hunter. With the men."

"Ah! Manly pursuits," Angerman said. "Well, we're men, too, right? Let's go find 'em." He gave Teddy Bear a joshing punch in the shoulder.

Teddy Bear grinned with delight. "Okay."

"Come on. And say your times tables as we go. Teacher

asked me to make sure you're practicing." He lied.

With a gulp, Teddy Bear began, "Two times two is seven times two is four times two is," while they headed off to find Hunter and Action Figure.

Angerman remembered seeing Hunter hurrying away from breakfast in the direction of Entrance East. Leading the way, he and Teddy Bear marched through the mall and out the doors into the parking lot on the east side.

The heat of the sun stopped them in their tracks for a heartbeat. The interior of the Crossroads was hot and stuffy, but out on the cracked black pavement, the heat and glare were intense. Gulls flapped down onto derelict cars and then screeched away again from the burning metal. Angerman raised a hand to shade his eyes and surveyed the area. Far to the left there were loading docks and the utility area for the mall. He could see men's figures moving about.

"There they are," Teddy Bear said at the same time Angerman noticed them.

Together, they made their way across the parking lot, where tall light poles towered like branchless trees. Somebody—the men of the Crossroads, maybe—had pushed or rolled the abandoned cars clear in a section where the light post had a faded sign, B7. In the midst of the cleared area was a soggy mass of ashes and paper. It looked like burned books. Teddy Bear ran toward it with a breathless exclamation that he might find something there for Teacher. Angerman went on under the beating sun to where the men were working with the horses.

Angerman stopped a little distance away, watching. An empty tractor-trailer had been converted into stables, and another held what looked like sacks of feed. Some of the men were grooming the four horses; some were making repairs to the chariots. Hunter was standing with the man who had given the sermon the night before in the theater. Now the man was showing Hunter some part of the harness, and Hunter was nodding, listening, eager to be accepted. Then he looked up and saw Angerman. His smile froze.

"Hey," Angerman called out. He walked forward. "Isn't Action with you?"

"No," Hunter said with such finality that Angerman halted.

The men were beginning to turn around, looking at the new arrival. One of the horses stamped a hoof, and the others twitched their ears at flies. The men's expressions were not exactly hostile but not welcoming, either.

I don't think they like you, Bad Guy whispered in Angerman's ear.

"He was fooling around, acting like a dumb kid. I don't know where he is," Hunter added.

"Got new glasses, I see."

"Yeah." Hunter put his hand to his face, and then dropped it. "Yeah, they work good."

All the pretty little horsies, a red one and a black one and a—

Angerman looked from Hunter to the preacher man, who was watching the conversation in silence. The man was staring at him now, his forehead creased. "Well, I guess I'll just go find him, then."

"Okay," Hunter said with obvious relief. "See you later."

There's four of them, did you notice? Four pretty horsies.

Angerman turned away, almost stumbling in his rush to get away before Bad Guy began shouting. As he hurried back toward the entrance, Teddy Bear ran to catch up with him.

"Found some good stuff for Teacher," Teddy Bear said with a proud smile. He was grimy with soot.

"Great, that's great," Angerman muttered. He put his shoulder to the door and pushed, barging inside.

Teddy Bear was trotting to keep up, and held out a soggy, half-burned booklet that flapped as he ran. "It's got pictures *and* words."

Hunter is going to be one of them, but not you, Nonono! You're not ONE OF THEM, are you! Bad Guy let out a high-pitched scream of laughter.

"See?" Teddy Bear said, flapping the charred pages. "It's maps. Maybe it's a secret treasure map."

"Yeah, fine." Angerman turned, not caring where he went or whether Teddy Bear was still keeping up with him. He kept his head down, counting tiles, and when he glanced up it was to see a whole shop full of Bad Guys standing around in their new clothes. He smothered a cry and turned down a corridor he hadn't explored yet.

"Hey, look," Teddy Bear said.

Angerman was almost afraid to turn to see what the boy was pointing at, but he raised his eyes. It was Action Figure, standing in front of a shop window. Angerman let all his breath out in a loud *whoosh.*

"Hey, kiddo, we've been looking for you," he called out.

Action Figure didn't answer. When they joined him at the window, he still had his eyes locked on something inside. The moment they reached his side he pointed.

"Whassit say?"

"What's what say?" Angerman lowered his head to Action Figure's level so he could sight along the boy's finger. In front of them was a large jar whose label showed a glistening, muscle-bound man flexing his biceps.

"Whassit say?" Action Figure demanded again.

Teddy Bear looked smug. "You shoulda done School. You shoulda learned the Baby-Sees with me and Baby and Doll."

"Shuh-up."

Angerman straightened. "It says *Man Power*. It's something you eat to make a great big man out of you," he said with a dry laugh.

"Man Power," Action Figure repeated.

Maybe you should take some of that, be one of the Men, Bad Guy whispered.

"Wanna come with us?" Angerman said, already moving away. "We're taking a walk."

He didn't bother to check if either of the boys was following. He didn't even care. All he cared about was getting someplace private where he could take the mannequin out of the backpack and thrash it against something hard.

The purple nail polish was already ruined. Teacher began picking at the smeared part on her left thumb, where the sticky paint was turning bumpy and hard. She tried not to let Cory's sneaking upset her, but inside she was shaken, and she saw her fingers shake, too. She would have to make sure Cory never got close to

The Book again. That girl could not be trusted.

Mommy was putting fancy white barrettes into Baby's hair, but they kept slipping out. "Oww!" Baby shrieked as one stray hair became caught in a clip.

"Sorry, Baby, but they won't stay in," Mommy said.

The little girl pouted and struggled out of Mommy's grip, running to where Doll was letting Ruth 2:10 put pale blue eye shadow on her lids.

"Me, too!" Baby pleaded.

"Mommy," Teacher said, keeping her voice down.

For a moment, Mommy kept her eyes on Baby and Doll, and Teacher saw that her expression was wistful, almost pained. At last, Mommy dragged her attention away. "What?"

Teacher hitched The Book higher onto her lap, to keep it from sliding off her knees. "Maybe we should see if Puppy and Kitty are up."

Immediately, Mommy sprang from the plush chair. She looked stricken. "How could I be so selfish? What was I thinking of? Ruth? Ruth! We're going to go get Puppy and Kitty. Can you tell us where—"

"Just a moment," Ruth 2:10 called out in a serene voice. She patted Doll's hair and kissed her forehead. "Perfect. A real angel. Now, what is it?" she asked, her white tunic billowing as she crossed the bridal shop.

Teacher tucked The Book under her arm as Mommy beckoned to the girls. "We want to see Puppy and Kitty," Teacher said, lifting her chin in a gesture of defiance. "It's almost lunchtime. They must be up by now."

"That's right," Mommy chimed in. "Where's this children's dormitory you said they were sleeping in last night? Come *on*, girls!" she added, frowning at Baby and

Doll still playing with the makeup. Doll was trying to put eye shadow on her dolly's one working eye, and Baby was struggling to get it away from her.

At first, Teacher thought Ruth 2:10 was going to say no, give them another reason not to go to their little strays. But the moment of hesitation vanished.

"Well, let's see where they are, then," Ruth 2:10 said.

She led the way through the mall, turning to climb the stairs to Upper Level East. "We find that this is the quietest part of the Crossroads," Ruth 2:10 explained. "So much better for little ones to sleep."

Teacher glanced up as they entered under a sign that read WELCOME TO TOYS AND TALES. Her heart beat a little faster at the thought that there might be a children's book section in this store, but when they entered she saw that what used to be bookshelves had been emptied of their contents and pushed into one corner to make space. The area was occupied by cribs and bunk beds, and toys were scattered around the floor. Doll and Baby ran to a toddler-sized table-and-chair-set to play with some pink plastic horses. A woman Teacher didn't recognize was changing the sheets on one of the cribs.

"Puppy! Kitty!" Mommy called, hurrying forward.

"Hello, Sister Exodus 5:12," Ruth 2:10 said.

"Hello, Sisters," the other woman replied, tucking a pillow under her chin and slipping a brand-new pillow-case onto it.

Teacher and Mommy dashed from bed to bed, but they were all empty. "When did they get up?" Teacher asked. "Where'd they go?"

"Who?" Exodus 5:12 replied

"Puppy and Kitty!" Mommy said. Her voice was

high and strained. "Aren't they here?"

The two women exchanged glances. By instinct, Teacher tightened her grip on The Book.

"They dint sleep here," Doll spoke up. She held a pink horse in one hand and her dolly in the other, making them speak to each other. "Me and Baby asleeped here, but Puppy and Kitty dint. Someone took them away at nighttime."

Mommy and Teacher looked at Doll, stunned. Mommy ran to the little table and knelt down, putting her hands over the toys. "Doll. Listen to me. Are you playing a Let's Pretend or is that really what happened?"

"People came and looked at them and took them away while me and Doll were asleeping but not really," Baby explained. "We weren't all the way asleeping yet."

Teacher scowled at the women. "What's going—"

"They were feverish," Exodus 5:12 said. "We checked on them and it turned out that they were both very sick. We thought it would be best to quarantine them, because we had no way of knowing what they had."

"Then I should be taking care of them!" Mommy said, her voice almost wild with worry. "Where are they? Why won't you let me see them?"

Ruth 2:10 tried to put her arms around Mommy and hold her, but Mommy wriggled away. In a flash, Ruth 2:10 took Mommy's wrist in a grip that wasn't so easy to shake.

"Calm down, now. They'll be fine. You have to stop worrying about them—"

"But they're—"

"They're not really your babies, after all," Ruth 2:10 said, her voice still kind and understanding. "You don't have to do it all on your own anymore. There are people here who are much older and more experienced than you about these things. You must trust that we know what we're doing. You don't want to jeopardize their health any further, do you?"

Teacher saw the color drain from Mommy's face, and she whirled around on Ruth 2:10 in anger. "That's a mean thing to say!"

"No, she's probably right," Mommy said, her chin quivering. "I don't really know how to take care of them the right way. I don't really know anything about how to be a mommy."

"There, now, see?" Ruth 2:10 released Mommy's wrist. "Let us worry about them for a while. When they're better you can play with them again. Now, when you've finished sulking, you can join us for the Communal Midday Meal."

Teacher was so stunned she couldn't speak. The two women left the children's dormitory, and Mommy lowered herself into one of the little chairs beside Baby and Doll. Instead of a responsible, tender, brave mommy who looked after a whole family, she had been turned into a useless child.

"This is bad," Teacher said. She pressed The Book to her chest even tighter, as if to stop everything from breaking apart. "This is really, really bad."

Chapter Six

It was almost time for the nightly meeting. Hunter hurried down the hall to Cine-Theater 6. He'd made a lot of progress with the Keeper men during this morning's Daily Strengthening, and he didn't want to blow that by being late.

"Hunter!"

Hunter stopped and turned around. Teacher was standing in the dark doorway of Crystal Sensations. She was holding a small candle in her hand.

He walked up to her. "What are you doing here? We'll be late for the meeting."

Teacher grabbed his arm and pulled him inside. "We have to talk. Come on."

She took his hand and led him to the back of the store. As they moved through the darkness, the light from her candle illuminated crystal unicorns, crystal balls, small pieces of rose quartz and amethyst and agate. Seeing the shiny, sparkling trinkets, Hunter was reminded of something from the Before Time: going caving with his First Daddy, moving through the cool, clammy darkness, the beams of their clunky flashlights winking off tiny pinpricks of brightness on the walls.

"Over here!"

Teacher pulled him behind the cash register. Hunter saw that Mommy and Angerman were sitting on the floor. "W-what are you guys doing?" he stammered.

"We're having our own little meeting," Angerman explained with a smile. He picked up Bad Guy, who was lying on the floor beside him, and propped him up on his lap, like a doll.

Hunter stared. With Bad Guy's face right next to Angerman's like that, Hunter thought he could see a resemblance between them. The same creepy smile.

He forced himself to tear his eyes away. "Where're Teddy and Action and the girls?"

"I asked Ruth if they could go to the Children's Dormitory and rest while the meeting was going on," Mommy explained. "I said they were tired."

"And what about us? Aren't the Keepers going to miss us?" Hunter pointed out.

"We can slip into the meeting a little late," Teacher said.

Hunter frowned and sat down, scrunching up against the hard side of the counter. "Okay, so what's up?" he said, trying not to sound too irritated.

"Let us call this meeting to order!" Angerman cried out. He squeezed Bad Guy's neck from behind and made the mannequin nod its head up and down. "Brothers and Sisters, amen!"

"Cut it out, Angerman," Teacher hissed. She sat down next to Hunter and cradled The Book in her lap. "We think there's something really weird going on in this place," she began.

"What? What do you mean?" Hunter asked her, surprised.

"They've separated us," Teacher explained. "The

little ones have to sleep in the Children's Dormitory, and we have to sleep in the futon store. The men took you aside, Hunter, to help take care of the horses, but they didn't ask Angerman or Teddy or Action."

"But—" Hunter protested.

"And where are Puppy and Kitty?" Teacher went on. "The Keepers won't let us see them!"

"Ruth says they're sick and can't see anyone," Mommy said in a small voice.

"Even if that's true and they have to be kept in isolation, Ruth could let us see them from a distance," Teacher said. "Through a window or a doorway or whatever."

Mommy's lip trembled. "I don't know," she whispered.

Hunter pushed his glasses up his nose. Things were so clear to him now; he wished things could be clear for the rest of the family, too. "I think we should give this place a chance," he said. "It's safe, it's clean, there's food, there are Grown-ups to take care of us. I'm sure the strays are fine," he added, glancing at Mommy. "I'm sure there's a good explanation."

Angerman leaned forward so that his face was just a few inches from Hunter's. "But don't you think these people are a little strange, Hunter dude?" he demanded. "Or are you becoming one of them? What were you doing with those men at the loading dock this morning, anyway?"

Hunter pulled back, startled. He didn't want to share with the others how much he had enjoyed the Daily Strengthening, had enjoyed being in the company of men. "Look, I learned some stuff about them. There's some guy called Supreme Leader, he's in charge of everything."

"You mean Duderonomy?" Teacher asked him.

Hunter shook his head. "No, someone different. This guy, Supreme Leader, pulled everyone together after Fire-us. Although they don't call it that here. They call it 'the Great Flame.'"

Angerman made Bad Guy nod again. "Very catchy name!"

"Where is this Supreme Leader?" Mommy asked Hunter. "Why haven't we seen him around?"

"He doesn't live here," Hunter said. "He lives somewhere else. They didn't say where."

"Allrighty, listen," Angerman said, sitting up a little straighter. "Seriously. Don't you think it's a little weird that there are so many Grown-ups here? If they're all so immune, why didn't we ever see any immune Grown-ups out there before? And who is this Supreme Leader guy? How did he manage to set all this up? This nice, cozy Food Court and Banana Republic life, when all the other Grown-ups in the world got sick and burned up and died horrible, terrible, intestine-boiling deaths?"

"Stop it, stop it," Mommy moaned.

"My point is . . . we should get out of here," Angerman said. "We should get out, continue on our journey, and find President. Just like we planned back in Lazarus."

Teacher nodded. "I agree with Angerman."

Hunter squirmed. He didn't like where this discussion was going. Maybe there was some reason to be concerned about Puppy and Kitty. And maybe the Keepers *were* a little odd. But the life here was so much better, a hundred times better, than being out there with the hot sun and the alligators and the washed-out bridges and everything else. "Can't we just wait and see?" he pleaded. "Maybe this Supreme Leader guy could give us some answers. He's alive—we don't even know if President is alive."

Angerman began to speak, but Teacher cut him off. She held up The Book. "Obviously we need some answers," she said. "After the meeting, the other meeting that is, I will put this under my pillow and pray for a dream. By morning, I will have an answer for our family. The Book will tell us what to do."

The mall was silent and nearly pitch-black. At Before-Midnight, which was when everyone was supposed to go to sleep, all the torches were extinguished except for one or two at each of the entrances.

Cory moved through the atrium with slow, careful steps, swinging her camping lantern from right to left. The candle inside it, the one she'd gotten from Wix 'n' Stix the Place for Candles, filled the air with a thick, sweet-flower smell.

Which flower was it? Cory lifted the lantern closer to her face. She could hardly remember any of the flower names. Roses, violence, lilies of the valley of the shadow of death. Her mama had loved flowers, and was always planting things in their garden, calling the flower names out to Cory and Ingrid as if they were the words to songs.

Ingrid. Cory's chest tightened with grief at the thought of her big sister. Where was she now? Was she still alive? Cory had been thinking about her ever since the morning's incident in Danielle's Bridal Shoppe, and had been unable to concentrate on anything else: the Daily Meditations, the Lessons, her numerous chores, the communal meals. Which had been difficult, because they had watched her extra-closely all afternoon and evening. And at tonight's meeting, Deuteronomy 29:28 had given an especially piercing sermon about the path of the just, and she could swear he had been looking at her the entire time.

The path of the just is not my path! Cory had wanted to shout to him, to everyone. But she knew there would have been consequences, terrible consequences, and so she had just kept her mouth shut.

But it was okay, because she knew her true path now, or at least a part of it. Those words—*Puppy says Ingrid wants more lemonade*—were a message to her. They told her that the twins who had come with Teacher and the others—Puppy and Kitty—were Ingrid's twins. She couldn't even remember what Ingrid had called them. The Keepers didn't give babies names, but Ingrid used to call them sweet names like Angel or Precious in secret. So their names were Puppy and Kitty now. That was fine with her.

And they were missing. Cory had overheard Mommy asking Ruth 2:10 about them once, twice, three times, only to have Ruth 2:10 respond with her usual vague, honey-toned excuses: *Don't you worry about them, now. They're fine. Everything is fine!*

Cory clenched her fists. Everything was *not* fine. She had to find Puppy and Kitty as soon as possible—*that* was her true path, or part of it. There might be more messages in the book in addition to the one she'd seen. She would have to take another look at it, which would not be easy.

The flower candle flickered, threatened to go out, and then steadied itself again. Cory realized that she had reached the intersection of two hallways. To her left was the Maternity Plus! store. In the dim light, Cory could just make out the familiar mannequin in the window. The mannequin had short blond hair but no eyes, no nose, no mouth, no expression whatsoever. Under the black jacket and skirt, her stomach was as big and round as the moon. Like Ingrid's used to be, right before the twins came.

Cory loves touching her sister's belly, which is surprisingly solid with the babies inside. She loves watching the skin of it ripple and roll with the babies' kicks. Sometimes, she can even make out the shape of one of the babies' feet stamped against her sister's belly. They're going to play for the Dolphins, Ingrid would say with a laugh, as if normal things like football still existed.

It is a happy time, after two years of much unhappiness. Two years before, Mama and Papa died in a car accident, and Ingrid had to raise Cory all alone. Then one day Ingrid packed all their things and said, Honey, we have to leave, and she and some friends of hers with weird names like Romans and Acts brought Cory to a special underground place.

Then the Great Flame happened, and everyone in Jacksonville except the Keepers of the Flame burned up and died. And maybe everywhere else, too—Cory was never sure about that. Cory, Ingrid, and the others in the underground place—a lot of grown-ups and a handful of children—were moved to the Crossroads Mall. On the way, Cory saw horrible things, dead bodies and overturned cars and burned-up buildings. Cory screamed and sobbed the whole way, upsetting the horses and some of the grown-ups, and Ingrid had to hold her and whisper, Close your eyes, just close your eyes, it's better not to see.

At the Crossroads Mall, it was a brand-new life. There was a man who was in charge, who even Deuteronomy 29:28 was afraid of, named Supreme Leader. Supreme Leader gave Ingrid a new name, Lamentations 1:2, and he gave Cory the name Corinthians 1:19. Cory slipped and called Ingrid "Ingrid" once in a while, but whenever that happened there would be consequences, so she quickly learned.

In the spring of that first year, Ingrid's belly started growing bigger. In the late fall, the babies came. They were beautiful babies, and Ingrid and Cory loved them so much. Other women at the Crossroads had babies that year, too, and in the following years. The halls were soon filled with cries and shrieks, happy sputtering noises, the slapping of palms against tile as the babies learned to crawl.

But after the first babies learned to walk and talk, the Testing began. Ingrid stopped being happy and started acting dark and rebellious and secretive. She wouldn't answer to her name, Lamentations 1:2 anymore. She wouldn't obey the older Keepers. And then one night, she disappeared with the twins.

The next morning, Cory was awakened before dawn and interrogated by Deuteronomy 29:28 himself. Where did she go? Where is Lamentations 1:2? they all shouted at her. Cory had no idea. For months, she cried every night, into her pillow in the Children's Dormitory.

Search parties in the chariots went out to look for Ingrid. The men carried crossbows. But even after months of searching, they weren't able to find Ingrid or her children. . . .

Cory's candle began flickering again. She realized that her hands were trembling, that she was shaking all over. She took a deep breath and willed herself to be calm. She had to focus on her mission. She had to find Puppy and Kitty before the Keepers realized that she was missing from her bed.

She continued down the hall, past the Limited and the FunZone arcade and Picture Perfect Frames. She stopped at each one, swung her camping lantern around, and peered inside. No sign of the twins. Once she was done with this hallway, she would have covered the entire first floor of the mall. She hoped she could cover the second floor before sunup.

There was a noise. It was the faintest noise, coming from somewhere up ahead. Cory halted in her tracks and stood very still. It took her a second to figure out that it was the soft sound of barking—from the direction of the pet shop.

But there were no dogs at the pet store. All the dogs and cats died years ago, when the pet food ran out and the Keepers didn't want to feed them human food.

Her heart hammering in her chest, Cory ran through the darkness toward the pet store. By the time she got to the entrance, the barking had stopped. Cory held the camping lantern high in the air and walked in.

It was pitch-black inside. Cory moved with deliberate slowness, first down one aisle and the next, barely noticing the shelves full of dusty aquariums, plastic seaweed, catnip balls, hamster wheels.

Way in the back, there were metal cages where the dogs and cats used to be. There were still signs taped up on some of them: GOLDEN RETRIEVER PUPPIES MARKED DOWN FROM $500 TO $250! TAKE THIS PERSIAN PUREBRED HOME FOR CHRISTMAS!

In one of the cages, Cory noticed several cat skeletons—or were they dog skeletons? Remembering the dead bodies from five years ago, all over Jacksonville, Cory felt nausea wash over her, the bitter taste of bile in her throat. She kept going.

The light of her camping lantern fell on the next cage. Cory clamped her hand over her mouth to keep from screaming. There was a small boy and a small girl huddled together in the corner, on top of old newspapers and sawdust shavings. The cage was locked with a padlock.

Cory was overcome with relief and happiness. And fury, pure fury. "How dare they put you in a cage?" she moaned. She fell to her knees and reached one fingertip through the metal bars. The twins stared at her with identical golden-brown eyes and began whimpering in fear.

"It's okay," Cory said in a soft voice. "It's okay. I'm going to help you." She smiled. "Listen, I need to know. This is important. Is your mama's name Ingrid?"

The boy blinked at her and said, "Yes."

Cory choked back a cry.

The girl blinked at her, too, and reached one stubby finger through the bars of the cage. She opened her mouth, as if to say something.

"What?" Cory whispered. "What is it, honey?"

The girl's finger curled around Cory's. "*We're still here*," she said.

Chapter Seven

Mommy burrowed down under the covers, trying to cling to the last shreds of sleep. Someone was moving about, rummaging. It sounded like Baby and Doll searching for something to wear, the way they always pawed through their piles of clothes, trying to come up with the perfect outfit. Ballerina tutu with baseball jacket or men's swimsuits topped with party dresses. *Have It Your Way!* they would chant, reciting their favorite one of the commandments. Mommy smiled, snuggling into the pillow.

Then she sat bolt upright. Her little girls weren't there.

It was Teacher making those sounds. She was tossing aside clothes, blankets, moving futon frames. She held up the battery-powered lantern in one hand. Her forehead was creased with a deep frown.

"I miss Baby and Doll." Mommy sighed. "I don't know why they have to sleep separate from us. And if I don't see Puppy and Kitty today I'll—I'll—"

Teacher paid no attention but kneeled on the floor, stretching her arm under Hunter's bed and feeling around.

"What is it?" Mommy said. She pushed the covers back and stepped out of her bed. The first glimmers of daylight were visible out in the atrium of the mall, but here in Futon-a-Rama, it was still dim.

Teacher raised the lantern over her head. It cast long, distorted shadows down her face. "I can't find it."

"Find what?"

Hunter stirred, rolling onto his stomach with a groan. Angerman kicked his legs out, and the covers made a muffled *flump* as he struggled in his sleep. Teacher watched the boys with a blank expression on her shadowed face, and then turned to Mommy. "The Book."

Mommy felt her heart swoop inside her ribs. "What do you mean?"

"The Book—it's not here anywhere," Teacher said. With trembling fingers she unzipped the fanny pack she'd begun using for keeping scissors and glue and pens in, as if the big bulky scrapbook could actually be in there.

Mommy felt dazed. "It has to be here—you never leave it."

Teacher thrust her arm under Hunter's pillow, bringing a grunt from him. She yanked it out again. "I didn't *leave* it. I had it when I went to sleep. Now it's not here."

"What's going on?" Hunter said, propping himself up. His hair was bent upward on both sides of his head, giving him the look of someone falling through space.

While Teacher continued rummaging through their things, Mommy drew the blankets around her shoulders. She shivered. "Teacher can't find The Book."

"By the Flame—" Hunter muttered.

"Don't say that!" Teacher whirled around on him, her eyes fierce. "Don't talk like them!"

"Huh? Why?"

Mommy shivered again. "Angerman! Wake up!"

In an instant, he threw the covers back and swung himself upright. "And now the news."

"Don't you start!" Teacher said. "Help me find The Book, you guys!"

Hunter stumbled around, groggy and addled from sleep. "I gotta go to the bathroom," he mumbled. "Where's my glasses?"

"Centers for Disease Control in Atlanta reports that outbreaks of the unknown virus have become so widespread as to call this a national epidemic," Angerman announced. His voice came out of the shadows where he sat. "Rioting has erupted at health clinics and hospitals in Seattle, Milwaukee, St. Louis, Miami, and Bethesda, and mayors of those cities have put in formal requests for the assistance of the National Guard. The national press corps is expecting an announcement from the White House, but the office of the President has not scheduled a press conference."

"Wait, not so fast," Teacher begged. "I gotta write this down, I don't have anything—"

Mommy noticed a tattered and half-burned booklet amid the debris: a road atlas. "How about this?"

Teacher snatched it from her. "Oh, good. Teddy found this yesterday," she said as she dug in the zippered pouch for a pencil and kept one eye on Angerman. "He's doing History."

Things were becoming a little crazy. Angerman was ranting, and Teacher was in a frenzy. Mommy felt the old screaming spirit that used to swarm through her, especially when she had to go outside for anything. Panic. Don't panic. But where were the children? Where were Puppy and Kitty?

"Our correspondents in London, Johannesburg, Tokyo, Bombay, Caracas, Sydney report the epidemic widespread in those countries Berlin, Paris, Cairo, Jakarta, Moscow, Istanbul report the epidemic widespread in those countries rumors are spreading as fast as the disease rumors of deliberate release of the virus—"

Angerman hauled himself from his bed as he spoke, dragging Bad Guy behind him by a length of telephone cord tied around its neck. He stood over Teacher, while she wrote furiously in the margins of the half-burned atlas. She flipped a page, and by the lantern's light Mommy saw a red winged horse in the corner. Angerman saw it too, or else something else made him scream so loud that Teacher jerked backward. He began pacing, slamming one fist into the other hand, and his face was distorted with some horrible emotion.

"'And there went out another horse that was *red:* and power was given to him that sat thereon to take peace from the earth,' you see? You see? 'And that they should kill one another: and there was given unto him a great sword'—but swords come in many shapes and sizes, don't they? DON'T THEY?" he yelled, yanking on Bad Guy's cord.

The mannequin bumped and smacked into the edge of Mommy's bed, and she shrank backward in fear.

"Two can play at that game," Angerman said in a voice full of hatred. He grabbed the mannequin's left arm and began wrenching it off.

"Please! Angerman!" Mommy forced herself to stand up and take him by the shoulders. She could feel how tightly he was wound up. He felt like stone. He finished breaking off one arm, and tackled the other while she tried to calm him. "Angerman, don't get crazy now! We need you. Puppy and Kitty need you."

He relaxed a fraction, and raised his head to look at Mommy. "There are Bad Guys all over this place. Everywhere," he whispered.

She looked down at the mutilated dummy and shuddered inside to think how dreadful it must be for him to see the stores full of mannequins. "I know, I know there are," she murmured. "Lots of Bad Guys."

"So we gotta go."

"Wait, wait, wait," Hunter broke in. "Not so fast."

"No, I think he's right," Mommy said. She pushed Angerman down onto a futon, where he sat in silence, glaring at Bad Guy. "How can we trust these people? See what's happening to us? I think this place is all wrong."

Hunter let out a groan and shoved his hands back through his hair. "Okay, look. We'll make them give us Puppy and Kitty today. They can't say no. They're nice people. We'll tell them that we can take care of Puppy and Kitty here—it'll be fine."

There was a patter of bare feet from outside. Mommy's heart leaped and she looked around with a smile of pure relief. It faded only slightly as Baby and Doll ran into the store in their nightgowns.

"We wanna sleep with you—we don't like that doorman-tory," Baby said, jumping up onto Mommy's futon.

"Sides," Doll went on. She settled herself backward into Mommy's lap. "Those Grown-ups keep asking us about Ingrid, but we don't even know anybody called Ingrid."

Mommy hugged Doll and pressed her face into the girl's hair. "That's silly. Why should they think you do?"

"Ingrid?" Teacher's voice had a strange edge to it. "They're asking about Ingrid?"

Surprised, Mommy looked up at Teacher through Doll's curls. "Do you know who it is?"

"Well, it's just that—" Teacher glanced out at the atrium and then at Mommy and the others. "There was something in The Book—about Puppy and Ingrid. It said Puppy says Ingrid wants more lemonade."

Cold swept up Mommy's back. "How can that be? How can Puppy be involved with someone named Ingrid, and how could it be in The Book? He couldn't have said anything about someone called Ingrid, he doesn't talk. Kitty doesn't talk."

"All I'm saying is, there's a sentence in The Book about Puppy and Ingrid, and that's what that girl Cory was reading yesterday when she was looking at it," Teacher explained with another worried glance at the door.

"Okay, that's it," Mommy said. She set Doll down with a thump and stood up. "We're getting Puppy and Kitty and we're getting them now."

Hunter half ran, half walked, trying to keep up with Mommy and Teacher and tuck his shirt in at the same time. Alternating waves of hot and cold broke across him like waves on the beach. It was so embarrassing! If only he had a chance to talk to the men first, he'd be able to explain how things were, how Mommy was so dedicated to the children and all. But now they were all just going to break in and make a scene, and he'd end up looking like a dumb kid.

"Where is everyone?" Teacher said as they stormed into an empty Food Court.

"Maybe there's a morning meeting. Let's check the theater," Mommy suggested. "We'll interrupt if we have to."

"Look, you don't have to get so excited," Hunter pleaded with them. "We'll just tell them how we want to see Puppy and Kitty."

Mommy stopped and whirled around so suddenly that Hunter nearly bowled her over. "Don't you think that's what we've been doing?"

Angerman, holding Baby and Doll by the hands, met them as they swung around through the atrium again. As usual, Bad Guy was in the pack on his back. "Where is everyone?" he asked.

They strode toward the theater, their heels clicking on the tiled floor. "We're looking for them now," Teacher said.

The drone and babble of voices reached them as they rounded the corner to the Cine-Theater 6 complex. The white-garbed women passed by them in a stream, and Hunter saw the mass of blue that was the men, all standing around Deuteronomy 29:28. A fresh stab of embarrassment shot through Hunter's stomach. He'd missed another meeting, obviously. They'd never think he was really one of the men, now.

"Hey, Dude-eronomy," Angerman called out.

The men with the minister formed a phalanx around him, and they all faced the kids square on.

"If you're the person in charge, then I have a complaint," Mommy said in a loud, clear voice. "We keep asking to see Puppy and Kitty, and the women keep making excuses to keep them from us. We want to see them."

Deuteronomy 29:28 signaled to someone behind Hunter, and he turned to see Ruth 2:10 making her way back to the theater entrance. She came to stand beside Deuteronomy 29:28.

"We're not trying to make trouble," Hunter hastened to say. He looked from one man to another to another, hope fading by the second as he met their stony stares. "We just want to see them."

"Fine." Deuteronomy 29:28 gestured to the men to leave and then turned to the kids again. "Wait here. I'm sure Ruth 2:10 will be happy to bring them to you."

Hunter almost laughed with relief. "See?" he said, turning to the others. "I told you it would be okay."

"Just wait inside," Ruth 2:10 said, ushering them into the theater.

"Why do we have to go in here?" Baby asked as she took Mommy's hand.

"It's just for a few minutes," Mommy said.

The doors shut behind them. The torches were still lit along the walls, flaring their red light and smoke up against the high ceiling. While Baby and Doll began a game running between the seats, Teacher beckoned the others near.

"I vote we leave," Teacher began. "As soon as they bring Puppy and Kitty, I say we should just get back on the road."

Angerman raised his hands into the air. "Hallelujah amen."

"I agree," Mommy said.

There was an uncomfortable silence. Hunter stared

at the floor, noticing the stains on the carpeting of the aisle. "Okay," he said in a low voice. For one awful moment he thought he might cry, but maybe it was the smoke that made his eyes sting so sharply. "You're right. You're right; I know you're right. I was trying to make it work out, but it's just—"

"It's just that these people are crazier than I am," Angerman said. He let out a wry laugh. "So let's figure out what our plan should be."

"I gotta find The Book," Teacher said. "That's number one. I bet that girl Cory snuck in last night and stole it—she's been so crazy about seeing it. Somebody should go get the boys, and then when we meet back here we'll get ready to go."

"I'll get them," Hunter offered. He met Mommy's gaze, and offered her a weak smile. "I'm okay. I'll get Teddy and Action, and we'll be ready to leave."

"We'll wait here for those guys to bring Puppy and Kitty," Angerman said.

"Okay then, let's go." Teacher strode up the aisle, and Hunter trotted to catch up.

"Do you think you can find her?" he asked as they pushed open the door.

"I'll find her," Teacher said with a grim look in her eyes. "And I'll make her give me The Book."

She headed off toward the Entrance West, and Hunter made for the stairs to the second level. At the landing, he was surprised to see Teddy Bear sitting on a bench, trying to open a plastic box with a yellow water pistol inside.

"Hey, I'm looking for you," Hunter said. "Where's Action?"

"In bed," Teddy Bear said, straining at the stiff plastic bubble of the package.

"In bed?" Hunter paused with one foot on the steps. "He's still asleep?"

"I dunno," Teddy Bear said without looking up. "I woke up when I heard the horses. I thought they might get loose and trankle me."

"They're outside—they can't trample you," Hunter said. His mind was running ahead, trying to sort out all that they'd need to get together. Food, supplies, water. And why was Action Figure still asleep? He turned back to look at Teddy Bear again, struck by a sudden thought. "What were the horses doing?"

Teddy Bear finally ripped open the plastic and tugged the water pistol out of its packaging. "Two men hooked up the chair-tiots to the horses and went gallumping away."

Hunter frowned. "Two chariots? Did you actually see two chariots?"

"I looked out the window," Teddy Bear said as though it was all perfectly obvious. "Two chair-tiots drove away real fast. A white horse and a gray horse."

Fear seized Hunter. "They didn't have Puppy and Kitty with them, did they?"

Teddy Bear stared at him wide-eyed. "No. They gallumped away real fast going toward that city we saw— Jack and Jill. But they didn't have Puppy and Kitty."

"Okay, listen," Hunter said. He wanted to snatch the toy away from Teddy Bear, make the kid see how serious this all was. "You remember the movie theater where we went to the meeting? Mommy is there. You go there and wait with Mommy."

"Is Teacher there?" Teddy Bear asked, beginning to look frightened by Hunter's tone.

"She'll be there in a minute. You go there and wait for her with Mommy. I have to wake up Action." Hunter waited, and then pulled Teddy Bear off the bench. "Go now."

When he saw that Teddy Bear was actually going down the stairs, Hunter turned and sprinted up the last steps to the second floor. The children's dormitory was straight ahead. He ran inside, scanning the beds and cribs. In the far corner, he saw Action Figure's red knapsack. "Hey, Action!"

Hunter dodged between cots and reached his brother's side. Action Figure was still asleep, and a thin sheen of sweat coated his forehead. Hunter jostled the boy's shoulder. "Come on, wake up. We gotta go."

"Whaaat?" Action Figure blinked, and turned his head from side to side.

"Come on," Hunter repeated, pulling back the covers. He reached down to grab Action Figure's knapsack and swung it over his shoulder. "Time to wake up, kiddo. Let's go."

Action Figure struggled upright and stumbled after Hunter. "Where's my stuff?"

"I've got it," Hunter said without even looking back. "Just get moving."

Angerman sat as still as possible in a folded-down theater seat. If he kept still and quiet, maybe he wouldn't feel so overwhelmed by what was happening. Beside him to the right sat Bad Guy, reduced to a legless, armless torso and head confined to a backpack. On his other side, Mommy sat with her feet up on the seat ahead of her, biting her nails and staring into space. Baby and Doll were on the stage, acting out some kind of fantasy.

"We are the Keepers of the Flame!" Baby said with a dramatic sweep of her arms.

Doll held Angerman's battered old picture frame up to her face. "Keepers of the *Frame!*" she corrected Baby.

They sure know how to start good fires, don't they? Bad Guy said in a quiet, confidential voice. *By the flame!*

Angerman glanced at Bad Guy. "What?" he whispered.

"You go to Pisgah," Doll said to Baby. "Take the black horse and tell Sup-eam Reader it's time to take his test."

"No," Baby said, shaking her head. She crossed the stage and tapped Doll on the chest. "Not him. Puppy and Kitty gotta take the test."

Angerman felt the hairs rise on his arms.

Never did like tests. Bad Guy sighed.

Mommy pulled her feet down and stood up. "What did you say, Baby? What did you say about Puppy and Kitty?"

"They gotta take a test."

Ohhhh, boy.

Angerman stood, too. His heart was racing. "Did you see someone leave in a chariot, girls?"

"With a black horse," Doll said.

Mommy gripped the back of the seat in front of her to steady herself. "With Puppy and Kitty?"

Doll shook her head. "Uh-uh."

Up at the back of the theater, a door opened. Angerman and Mommy turned around to see one of the men come in. He paused inside the doorway. He was alone. Mommy made a movement, but Angerman gripped her arm to stop her.

"We've decided it is for the best that you not see the little ones," the man announced.

"That's not—"

Angerman jerked Mommy's wrist. "Okay!" he called in a cheery voice. "We understand. No problem."

The man turned and left, and the door thumped shut behind him.

"What's wrong with you?" Mommy gasped. "Don't you see what they're doing?"

"Yes," Angerman said. He looked up at the stage, where Doll and Baby were still acting out the conversations they had overheard among the women and men of the Crossroads. "And it's way more serious than we thought."

Chapter Eight

The storefront signs were a blur as Teacher ran down the hall. Out of the corner of her eye she saw *GIFTS 'N' something . . . AU something PAIN . . .* but the words made no sense to her—they were alien and strange. She had always loved words, had lived for them even. But now, without The Book, she had no way of comprehending their meaning. She might as well be blind, for it was like that—like some part of her had been cut away, rendering her useless. For the first time, she understood the wild, primitive grief Mommy felt when the little ones were taken from her, even briefly.

She wanted to kill Cory. Really kill her. Cory had The Book—that was obvious to her—but now Cory was missing. She hadn't been among the crowd leaving the emergency meeting, and there had been a great deal of whispering and buzzing among the Grown-ups: *Where is Corinthians 1:19? . . . She wasn't in her bed this morning. . . . She was supposed to report for Food Preparation Duty. . . . She had better have a good explanation, by the Flame! . . . She is supposed to have her final fitting today. . . .*

The fitting! Teacher stopped in her tracks. She hadn't checked Danielle's Bridal Shoppe yet. Maybe Cory was there now, getting pinned into that crazy white wedding dress. She turned and started running again, back toward the Food Court.

When Teacher got to Danielle's, she saw those Keeper women—Psalm 12 and Proverbs 3:21 and Micah 2:9—through the plate glass window. They were fussing over Cory's dress, which they had slipped over a headless mannequin. Psalm 12 had a pair of razor-sharp-looking scissors and was holding the blades near the neckline, ready to cut something.

Teacher walked through the door, the bottoms of her brand-new SkyFlite hightops slapping against the floor. The three women heard her and whirled around with expressions of white-hot rage. But when they realized it was Teacher and not Cory, their expressions turned immediately, identically bland.

"Sister, hello," Psalm 12 called out with a pleasant smile. The hand with the scissors dropped to her side. "What can we do for you?"

Teacher pushed a strand of hair out of her eyes. "I have to find Cory. Do you know where she is?"

Psalm 12's smile vanished. "Cory? Don't you mean Corinthians 1:19?"

Teacher opened her mouth to say, *Cory, Corinthians 1:19, whatever,* but stopped herself. The women looked so deadly serious. "Yes, Corinthians 1:19. Do you know where she is?"

"We were just wondering that ourselves," Micah 2:9 said.

Psalm 12 cocked her head. "Why are you so interested in finding her, Sister?"

"Sh-she has something of mine," Teacher stammered, fingering the fanny pack at her waist. She didn't want to explain about The Book.

Proverbs 3:21 waved a hand at the carpeted

footstool. "Why don't you sit there and wait for her?" she suggested. "She's supposed to be here any minute for her final fitting. You young girls can talk while we work on her."

"We could work on you, too, Sister," Micah 2:9 added, taking a few steps toward Teacher. "We didn't get a chance to finish your manicure yesterday. And we could do your makeup, too!"

"Yes, Micah 2:9. What a splendid idea!" Proverbs 3:21 cried out. She pulled a long makeup brush out of the pocket of her tunic. It left a powdery beige trail across the front of the white fabric. "'So shall the king greatly desire thy beauty: for he *is* thy Lord; and worship thou him,'" she quipped.

"By the Flame!"

"By the Flame!"

"How old are you, Sister?" Micah 2:9 asked Teacher.

Teacher started. Why did they want to know how old she was? What did these Keeper women want from her? She began backing up toward the door, trying to think of an excuse to leave.

"Where are you going, Sister?" Proverbs 3:21 asked her. "What about your manicure and takeover?"

"I have to go and, um, check on my little brother, Teddy." Teacher lied. "I'm sorry to bother you all. Goodbye!" With that, she turned on her heels and went running out into the hall.

She ran and ran, pumping her thin arms, not looking back. When she reached the far end of the atrium, she stopped and glanced over her shoulder. The women weren't following her, thank goodness, although there was a group of Keeper men standing just outside Sugar and Spice, staring at her. She turned away from them and kept walking down a side hall, pretending to ignore them.

The Keepers were so strange—everything here was so strange. Teacher knew she had to find Cory and get The Book back so the family could get out of here as soon as possible. How long would it take to find it? The rest of today? Today and tomorrow? *Call For A Free Estimate!* was one commandment she'd never understood. Call who? How? Who could tell her how long it would take? That was the sort of thing she would normally look in The Book for guidance on, but she didn't have The Book. That was the whole problem.

Just beyond, at Entrance North, there was a flash of red. It looked like a person, hugging the walls and scrunching up behind a tall, brown-leafed tree, as if he or she didn't want to be seen. After a moment, Teacher realized that the person was wearing a red shirt, a red plaid shirt. She gasped and broke into a run.

"Cory!" she yelled. "Cory, Corinthians, whatever your name is, you stop right there!"

To Teacher's surprise, Cory didn't try to escape. Instead, she stepped out from behind the tree and began running in Teacher's direction.

The two girls stopped in the middle of the hallway, panting, facing each other. Cory's eyes were bloodshot, and her face was streaked with tears. Her red shirt was rumpled, as though she had slept in it.

"I'm so glad I found you," Cory said in a hoarse, ragged voice. "I need to speak to you."

"I need to speak to *you*," Teacher snapped. "Where have you been? Everyone's been looking for you." Her gaze swept over Cory, searching for The Book—where was The Book? Cory's hands were empty, and she wasn't wearing a backpack or anything.

"I went to the place of my Visioning again," Cory whispered. "But nothing came to me. Please, I gotta look at your book again, 'cause I found—"

"*You* have The Book," Teacher hissed. "You stole it from me last night while I was sleeping. Where are you hiding it?"

Cory's eyes grew enormous. "You . . . you don't have your book?"

"I'm telling you, you stole it from me last night while I was sleeping!"

"I didn't steal it," Cory insisted. She gazed at some point over Teacher's shoulder. "They must have taken it. Ruth 2:10 or one of the other Keepers. Oh, Teacher, this is terrible," she whispered. "They burn books here, you know. They'll burn yours, if they haven't burned it already!"

"You're lying!" Teacher gasped.

"I am not lying—I am telling the truth!"

Teacher stared hard into Cory's eyes. She *was* telling the truth. Teacher pictured The Book going up in flames in the asphalt parking lot, the thick pages hissing and curling and turning black. All those words, disappearing forever. The Book was her family's past, her family's future. It was all they had besides each other, and they—she—could not survive without it.

Mommy repositioned herself so she could get a better angle on Doll's elaborate hairdo. It was dark in the Cine-Theater, just a few torches here and there, and Teddy

Bear had to shine a flashlight down on them. Doll had asked that her hair be braided into a single braid, "just like Coreethenee's," except that she had also wanted Mommy to add a handful of barrettes and ribbons from Danielle's Bridal Shoppe.

"Done yet, Mommy?" Doll clamored.

"My turn next!" Baby piped up from two seats over. She bounced up and down, making the velvety chair groan and squeak.

"Baby, sit still! You too, Doll. It's hard to get this ribbon tied when you're wriggling around like that! Move the light higher, Teddy—that's it, thanks."

Mommy busied herself with the work at hand—tying ribbons, snapping barrettes shut—and tried not to worry about what lay ahead. Hunter had gone and found Teddy Bear and Action Figure, and now the family was back in the Cine-Theater waiting for Teacher to come back with The Book. After which they would have to form a plan of action to find Puppy and Kitty and get out of here.

Her heart thumped in her chest at the thought of her two little babies somewhere in the mall. Were they really sick, as the Keepers had claimed? In any case, they were probably alone and scared and wondering if Mommy and the others had abandoned them. And since they couldn't talk, they wouldn't be able to ask for help. . . .

Brushing back a tear, she tugged at the ends of the bow and patted Doll's head. "There, you're all done. Baby, you ready for your pretty do?"

Baby jumped out of her seat and started elbowing Doll out of hers. "Get out, get out, it's my turn!"

"Stop it—you hurted me," Doll complained.

Mommy could see Hunter and Angerman in the corner, talking in hushed voices. She figured the boys were forming an escape plan. Angerman appeared distracted—he seemed to be addressing his comments to that awful mannequin in his backpack as much as to Hunter, and Hunter kept reaching over and grabbing Angerman's arm, as if to bring him back around.

Mommy wondered all of a sudden where Action Figure was. And then she noticed him, sprawled in a seat in the next row over. His arms were wrapped around his chest, and his eyes were fluttering open and shut. She was relieved that he wasn't acting like his usual self, racing around and knocking things down and causing trouble. He was taking a nap and being quiet, and that was a welcome change.

"Mommy, Mommy!"

Mommy glanced up. Teacher was weaving through the dark theater toward her and the little ones. Mommy waved at her and cried out, "Did you find it? Did you find The Book?"

Teacher knelt down in the aisle by Mommy's seat and shook her head. Even in the dim light, Mommy could tell that Teacher's face was ashen. Angerman and Hunter came over.

"I found that Cory girl, but she didn't have The Book," Teacher moaned. She opened the pouch at her waist and fingered through the burned maps inside. "She thinks the Keepers took it. She says . . . she says they burn books here."

"That's where I found you the maps, Teacher!" Teddy Bear piped up with a smile. "In the book barbecue pile!"

Teacher stared at her brother with a pained expression. "I . . . I suppose I should check that out, see if The Book might be . . ." Her words trailed off as she covered her face with her hands.

Mommy reached down and hugged her friend. "Don't worry, it's going to be all right, we'll find The Book. We *have* to." She glanced around at the others. Making her voice sound as strong and steady as possible, she said, "Let's make a plan, okay, everybody? We need to find The Book. We need to find Puppy and Kitty. We also need to collect supplies and stuff so we can get out of here."

"Angerman and I were talking. I can get bikes from that store, X-treme Byxx or whatever, and start stashing them someplace," Hunter volunteered. "Mommy and Teacher, you and Angerman should split up and look for The Book and the wild ones."

Teacher brushed away a tear. "All right, yes."

"Not to be a party-pooper, guys, but I just had a thought," Angerman spoke up. "How do we know those three chariots the kiddies saw didn't take Pup-Pup and Kitty-Kitty with them?"

"The strays weren't in the gray-horse chair-tiot or the white-horse chair-tiot," Teddy Bear said.

Doll held her Dolly up to her ear and nodded. "Uh-huh, right." She glanced up. "Dolly says it was just a big tall Grown-up in the black chariot."

"Puppy and Kitty must still be in the mall, then," Mommy said.

"This also means there's only one chariot and one horse here at the mall. The red one. Which means it'll be harder for the Keepers to follow us once they get wind of the fact that we're gone." Hunter put his hands on his hips. "Okay, let's get moving. Everyone meet back here as soon as our missions are accomplished. Baby, Doll, Teddy, Action . . . you stay here, don't move, and don't talk to anyone! If one of the Keepers shows up, just, uh, pretend to be taking naps or something. Understand?"

Baby nodded up and down. "Unnerstand."

Teddy Bear nodded, too. "Yessir, understand."

"Action's already taking a nap, not a pretend nap but a real asleeping nap," Doll said, studying her braid.

Mommy saw Hunter glance over at his brother, who was still sprawled back in his chair. Action Figure's eyes were closed, and he was tossing and mumbling. Hunter frowned.

Mommy tugged on Hunter's sleeve. "Hunter? What are we going to do if we run into the Keepers out there?" she whispered.

"We're gonna have to play along and act like we're one of them," Angerman spoke up. His head whipped around, and he grabbed the Bad Guy mannequin by the neck. "*Yes*, play along. Yes, *act* like we're one of them. Shuddup!"

"Angerman's right. We can't make them suspicious," Hunter said, glaring at Angerman. "Anyone see one of the Keepers, we're Keepers, too."

Teacher let out a harsh laugh. "By the Flame!"

Cory hovered in the doorway of the Tux Connection, watching and waiting for Teacher.

Teacher didn't know it, but Cory had followed her to the Cine-Theater 6. Teacher had been inside for a while now. Cory wondered if she should keep waiting, or if she should just march into the theater and try to talk to her again.

She closed her eyes. They hurt so much from no sleep and the crying, she wished she could just keep them closed like that and curl up on the floor. And rest.

Close your eyes, just close your eyes—it's better not to see.

Cory thought about Ingrid's babies, locked up in their cages at the pet store. She had been forced to leave them there overnight. She couldn't get the padlock undone, and besides, what would she do with them once she got them free? Ingrid had managed to escape the Crossroads with them three years ago, but could Cory do the same? Ingrid was so strong, so willful, so smart. What did she, Cory, know? She knew how to prepare the communal meals at the Food Court, and she knew how to sit still for manicures. She knew how to quote Scripture and be respectful, sort of, to the older Keepers, and she had been taught how to bow special to Supreme Leader for the time when she would meet him in the future. And that was about it.

She had told the twins that they had to be brave, that she would come back for them as soon as possible. And then she'd left the mall and walked, staggered really, to East Florida Precision Industrial Lenses. She was hoping for another dream to tell her what to do, how to save the twins, but nothing came to her.

Cory knew she had to get the twins out of the mall. They had been in danger three years ago, and they were in danger now. The question was, how? She was sure the answer was in Teacher's book.

Cory heard a noise. Her eyes flew open. Teacher,

Mommy, and those two boys—Hunter and Angry Man—were coming out of the Cine-Theater 6. Cory was just about to call out to them when she saw Ruth 2:10 heading down the hallway toward them. Cory retreated deeper into the doorway of the Tux Connection, out of Ruth 2:10's view.

"Hello, Sisters and Brothers," Cory heard Ruth 2:10 call out. "Where are you going?"

"We thought we'd do some shopping!" Cory heard Mommy reply in a cheerful voice.

The voices drifted away. Cory stuck her head out of the doorway. Just at that moment, Mommy walked into the Tux Connection.

The two girls started and stared at each other.

"W-what are you doing here?" Mommy demanded.

Cory grabbed her arm. "Please, I gotta talk to you. Where's Teacher?"

Mommy wrenched her arm away. "She's . . . shopping. What do you want?"

"I need to talk to you and your friends about the twins. The ones you call Puppy and Kitty," Cory explained.

Mommy's eyes grew cold all of a sudden. "I'm sure it's all for the best," she said. "I have complete trust in the older Keepers, by the Flame!"

Cory reached out and put her hand on a tuxedo-clad mannequin, for support. What was Mommy saying? Had she and Teacher and the others been converted by the Keepers? Cory mumbled something to Mommy, she wasn't sure what, and hurried out into the hallway. Ruth 2:10 was gone. Cory started walking in the direction of the pet store.

"Where are you going?" she heard Mommy call out to her.

"Shopping," Cory replied.

Cory prayed that she had the strength to do what she had to do.

Chapter Nine

There was a pull-down metal gate across the entrance to X-treme Byxx, but someone had pulled it up far enough to leave a three-foot gap at the bottom. Hunter took a quick look left and right, and then ducked under the gate. Brightly colored skateboards and high-tech scooters took up one whole wall of the shop, and fancy racing bikes and mountain bikes hung from hooks on the other walls, but there were also simple beginner bikes and bikes for kids. They stood in rows around the store, glinting faintly in the filtered light that came from the atrium. Hunter nudged back the kickstand on a mid-sized blue bike with chopper handlebars, perfect for Action Figure, and began threading his way toward the back where he could see a metal door marked Exit.

For a moment, he debated whether he should leave their getaway vehicles outside. But if someone spotted them before they were ready to escape, their plan would be spoiled. On the other hand, if the moment to flee arrived and then they all had to bump and jostle to get their bikes out the door, it might waste precious time. He chewed his lower lip. Then he nodded. Leaving them outside was too much of a risk. He pushed the bar-latch on the door, letting in a brilliant slice of sunshine, and let it close again without catching. Then he propped the blue bike against the wall beside the door and went back for more. As he passed a row of small kids' bikes, the thumb latch on a handlebar bell snagged on his shirt, and the entire row toppled over when he jerked away. Hunter froze, his eyes glued to the security fence and the atrium beyond. Seconds ticked by to the sound of his thudding heart, but nobody came, nothing happened.

With a small sigh of relief, Hunter went back to his task, selecting bicycles for every member of their family. Two adult-sized bicycles already had child-seats attached to them. He squinted in the dim light, and read *Children under 25 pounds*. There was no way of knowing how heavy Puppy and Kitty were. They were scrawny, but Hunter guessed they were probably too big for the baby seats.

On the other hand, there didn't seem to be much of a choice. When they had left Lazarus, they had the kind of wagon that hitched to the back axle of a bike, and the little ones rode in that. A quick glance around X-treme Byxx showed there weren't any of those in the store. The baby seats would have to do. Hunter wheeled both of those bikes toward the exit door to join the growing fleet.

A strange, echoing sound from the atrium halted him as he reached for a silver-gray racing bike for Angerman. Hunter listened, waited, breathed. It was the sound of voices echoing from the far end of the mall, a crowd of people talking but moving even further away. The sound faded out. Hunter lifted the silver-gray bike off its hook and wheeled it into place. It was the last one. All the others were there, including one with an air pump strapped to the frame and a pair of saddlebags on either side of the rear wheel. He had stuffed the saddlebags with flip-top water bottles, wraparound sunglasses, and caps with visors. He couldn't help smiling. Good hunting.

With a last look around the store, Hunter dug his jackknife from his pocket and punctured the tires of the remaining adult bikes. Down the rows he went, leaning down by each bike, then giving a quick stab front and back. No one would be able to chase them down, now.

He ducked back under the fence, and then turned to inspect the store. Nothing looked out of place if you didn't look too closely. With a nod of satisfaction, he turned and headed for Outdoor Outfitters two stores away, making a mental list: packs, tent, compass, freeze-dried food. There should be a whole treasure trove in the camping store, if the Keepers hadn't used it up themselves, yet.

Inside the store, Hunter grabbed a backpack first, and then began filling it as he went down the aisles: pouches of food, waterproof matches, candles, water purification tablets, nesting cook pots, first-aid kit, rain ponchos. When it was full he propped it up just inside the entrance and grabbed another pack. He strapped a dome tent in its carry bag to the bottom of the pack frame, and went back to the food aisle. How many backpacks? He could carry one, Teacher could carry one. Could they persuade Angerman to ditch his stupid Bad Guy and fill his pack with useful stuff? But what about the baby seats, would they be in the way? Was Teddy Bear strong enough to ride with a backpack? Deep in thought, Hunter placed the second loaded pack next to the first, and paused at the entrance.

"Brother! There you are!"

It was a man's voice. Hunter felt the muscles in his

back clench. He turned around slowly, edging away from the backpacks full of incriminating escape supplies. Striding toward him was Daniel 7:15. Hunter remembered him from Daily Strengthening: the guy was strong and a fast runner, too. It wouldn't be easy to get away from him if he had to.

"What's up?" Hunter asked, keeping his voice cheery. He took another step away from the backpacks. They were obscured by a display rack of fly-fishing vests.

"There's a very important meeting," Daniel 7:15 said. "All you kids from Outside are supposed to be there."

"Oh, sure. I'll be right there. I have to—"

Daniel 7:15 smiled. "Now."

"Right." Hunter tried not to be too obvious about swallowing the lump of fear that swelled his throat. "Okay."

Teacher tried not to let her imagination race ahead of her as she followed Acts 9:5 out through Entrance South. The summons had been so abrupt, so unexpected that Teacher hadn't been able to think of a way out of it. One moment she had been walking out of Tye-Dye Hut after searching it for The Book, and the next moment there was Acts 9:5 saying Teacher was ordered to attend a special meeting.

Through the second set of doors, Teacher could see the entire population of the Crossroads standing in a circle in the parking lot. There were plenty of rusted cars dotting the broad, black pavement, but in one area they had all been cleared away. This was where all the people were gathered. Through the human fence that blocked her view, Teacher caught glimpses of flames. She looked up over their heads and saw shimmering heat rising from the center of the crowd and trails of gray smoke. At once, her heart began to race.

"Over here," Acts 9:5 said with a gesture and a look that gave Teacher no choice.

Men and women parted to let her through, and Teacher found herself a place in the front ranks. Across from her, through the wavering haze of heat, she saw Mommy surrounded by women in white. A quarter of the way around the circle she saw Angerman, and across from him to her other side was Hunter. They were all there, separated from each other. Teacher was sure it was deliberate, but her mind was stumbling with wild thoughts and she couldn't grasp what the point was. Why keep them apart? To keep them from talking to each other? Had any of them found The Book? Or Puppy and Kitty? It was so *hot*.

Already she was sweating. The sun pressed down on her head and radiated off the parking lot into her feet, and the heat from the bonfire pulsed against her face. She raised a hand to wipe the dampness from her upper lip, wondering, dreading, what was coming next. The people were silent and expectant, their gazes focused on the fire. The only sounds were the snapping and popping of the flames and the hollow rattle of an empty soda can that rolled in fits and starts across the parking lot with the breeze.

"By the Flame," someone behind her whispered.

A murmur of assent rippled through the crowd, like fire spreading across paper. "By the Flame."

Teacher drew a deep breath and spoke for everyone to hear. "By the Flame."

On the far side of the circle, midway between Anger-man and Mommy, the crowd parted and Deuteronomy 29:28 stepped forward. All heads turned his way.

He raised his arms in a symbol of benediction. "Brothers and Sisters, this is a Good Day."

"By the Flame," replied the crowd in unison.

"Today we will dedicate our new Brothers and Sisters as members of our family."

Teacher saw people look at her with warm smiles, and she forced herself to smile back, as if this were the happiest day of her life. Someone patted her shoulder in encouragement. Teacher could feel the hairs on the back of her neck prickling.

"Remember!" Deuteronomy 29:28 said in a solemn voice. "Our old lives were nothing but sorrow and pain."

Teacher knew to respond in chorus as the crowd said, "By the Flame."

"But the World was made anew. God worked for six days, and on the seventh day he rested, and saw that it was Good. And the Chosen people burned their bridges to their old lives of sorrow, and dedicated themselves to the Great Future."

"By the Flame."

Deuteronomy 29:28 beckoned to Mommy and to Hunter and Angerman, and Teacher saw him beckon to her through the shimmer of heat and flames. With a stiff, halting step, Teacher walked out into the open and skirted the bonfire, joining the others in front of Deuteronomy 29:28. She tried to meet Mommy's gaze, but Mommy had her eyes locked on the preacher with a phony expression of reverence and calm. Hunter was looking around, smiling and nodding like a kid getting a football trophy at an awards ceremony. Angerman was grinning from ear to ear, but his eyes were wild. His lips moved as he spoke to himself, or to Bad Guy, too softly to hear. Bad Guy now had a leather dog leash wrapped around his neck. Teacher thought she was going to throw up.

Suddenly, Deuteronomy 29:28 reached out and placed his hands on Mommy's head. Teacher saw her try not to flinch.

"From now on you have a new name, which is Esther 2:17. 'And the king loved Esther above all the women, and she obtained grace and favor in his sight more than all the virgins; so that he set the royal crown upon her head, and made her queen instead of Vashti.'"

Mommy's smile was frozen in place. Teacher's stomach swooped and fluttered.

"By the Flame!" came a loud chorus from the crowd.

Deuteronomy 29:28 then turned to Hunter. "Little Brother, you are now Psalms 140:11. 'Let not an evil speaker be established in the earth: evil shall hunt the violent man to overthrow him.'"

"By the Flame," Hunter croaked.

Teacher braced herself as Deuteronomy 29:28 took a step toward her, and she could not help cringing inside as he put his hands on her hair. "Isaiah 34:11. 'But the cormorant and the bittern shall possess it; the owl also and the raven shall dwell in it: and he shall stretch out upon it the line of confusion, and the stones of emptiness.'"

"By the Flame," Teacher whispered.

"And lastly," Deuteronomy 29:28 said as he turned to Angerman.

"Dude," Angerman said in a faint voice. He was as

white as bone dust in spite of the intense heat.

A flicker of annoyance flashed over Deuteronomy 29:28's face, but he put a hand on Angerman's shoulder.

"Your name shall be Proverbs 6:27. 'Can a man take fire in his bosom, and his clothes not be burned?'"

Angerman's lips moved while the crowd intoned "By the Flame." Teacher strained to hear him.

"No," he was saying. "No, no, he can't, he can't."

No *what*? Teacher wondered. Who did he mean? She tried to move closer to him, but Deuteronomy 29:28 had not finished his ceremony.

"Now that you have put your old life behind you, you must show us that your heart is free from memories." Deuteronomy 29:28 turned to the man standing behind him and held out his hands for something. When he turned around again, Teacher felt her knees go weak.

He was holding The Book.

"Do you know what you must do?" he said, looking at Teacher. "Do you know what it means to burn your bridges?"

As if in answer, the bonfire let out a crackle of sparks. Teacher heard a sharp hiss of breath from Hunter. Beside her, Angerman was still muttering, "No, no, he can't, he can't."

Teacher stood as if turned to stone. In an instant, she saw herself as if from high above, a lightning-quick telescoping of space and time that showed her the fire and the ring of solemn Grown-ups and Mommy and Hunter and Angerman—and Deuteronomy 29:28 holding out the most precious thing in the world for her to throw into the flames. She heard the Bible verse that the man had given her for her name, and heard the phrase *stones of emptiness* echo in her heart.

"NO HE CAN'T!" Angerman shouted and time sped up again.

Before anyone could move, Angerman snatched The Book from Deuteronomy 29:28's hands, and began hopping from foot to foot, prancing away. As the men surged forward with angry shouts, Angerman whooped and screeched toward the fire.

"No! Wait!" Hunter called out, stepping forward and holding up his hands to halt the men. "He—he—" He cast a desperate glance back at Mommy and Teacher. Teacher was still too shocked to think.

"He gets like this sometimes!" Mommy blurted out. "He gets a little crazy, but he'll be okay."

"And the fire came down from heaven and touched the evil doers," Angerman babbled. "And burned them in their houses and in their cars and in their schools— and did you know the fire wasn't supposed to hurt little children because they're innocent of sin and even though they wanted to have real lives they couldn't, you see, you see 'cause everything was on FIRE! That's right! A man cannot take fire into his bosom and his kids not be burned! And now a word from our sponsor! Kids, have you tried catching stray animals to keep as pets? Then you know how hard it can be to tame such wild things and teach them commands. Buy a certified purebred cat or dog from Chaffee's Pet Barn where this week only we're having a two-for-one special car wax conditions and shines as it cleans. In other news today, the four horsemen of the Apocalypse were seen going into the White House for high-level talks with the President."

The Grown-ups stood in a stupefied silence as

Angerman danced around the bonfire with The Book, hollering and ranting. Many of them were staring at Bad Guy, who jumped and bounced in Angerman's backpack with every leap and kick. Teacher felt Mommy grip her arm, and she met Mommy's eyes. "Puppy and Kitty," Mommy said, forming the words silently.

With a gasp, Teacher looked back at Angerman, who was cavorting his way closer and closer to the mall entrance. The crowd parted, although some people made as if to bar his progress.

"We'll get The Book back from him," Teacher said, turning back to Deuteronomy 29:28. "We know how to handle him when he's like this. I'm sorry he interrupted the ceremony—it's been so special and wonderful and everything, getting new names, but we could even start over again and do it the right way."

Mommy and Hunter were already following Angerman into the mall, and Teacher began backing away from Deuteronomy 29:28, still explaining as she avoided the fire. "We just have to calm him down, it'll just take a second. We'll be right back," she promised, and then turned and ran.

As she burst into the atrium, she saw Angerman stuffing The Book down into his backpack beside Bad Guy. "It's down the north wing, first level," he said, his voice normal. "On the left side."

"Chaffee's Pet Barn. Got it." Mommy nodded.

"Then meet us inside X-treme Byxx, ground floor, west wing," Hunter said as he helped Angerman swing his pack into place again.

Mommy nodded again and sprinted away.

"You guys get the kids from the theater," Hunter

said. "I'll get the gear. Meet you at the bike shop."

"Right," Angerman said. He buckled the waist strap and gave Teacher a wry smile. "We better make it fast. No telling how much time we've got before they come after us."

"Angerman—" Teacher's throat closed with sudden tears. "I—"

"Yeah, yeah. You're welcome. Now let's get out of here."

Chapter Ten

Standing at the pet store entrance, Cory glanced right and left and
over her shoulder, to make sure no one had followed her.
The hallway was deserted. Good.

Her fingers tightened around the thing she had found
at X-treme Byxx, some sort of tool with a long metal
point. She had seen the men use it during the Daily
Strengthening, to fix the chariots. She hoped it would
work on the padlock on Puppy and Kitty's cage.

On her way out of X-treme Byxx, she had almost run
smack into that Hunter boy. She was glad she had
spotted him first and managed to slip behind the water
bottle display as he walked by. She couldn't trust him
anymore—not him, not Angry Man, not Mommy, not
even Teacher. The Keepers had gotten to them, that was
for sure.

Taking a deep breath, she entered the pet store. The
hair prickled on her arms . . . something was different.
Squinting to see in the dim light of the room, she realized
that there was a pile of dog leashes on the floor in front
of her. The rack with the leashes had been knocked
down, and someone had picked through them and left
them there, all tangled up like spaghetti.

Cory stepped around the pile and quickened her
steps—had the twins escaped somehow? Or had
someone been here recently, maybe one of the Keepers?

As she neared the twins' cage, she heard the soft

sound of singing: "Hushaby, don' you cry, go to seep my little babies!"

"Hello?" Cory called out.

The singing stopped. Cory walked over to the big cage. The acrid smell of urine—human urine—greeted her nostrils. Two pairs of eyes stared out at her.

The twins were huddled together way in back. Their faces were grimy and streaked with tears, and their brand-new GapKids outfits were stained yellow. Cory bit back a cry of outrage and gritted her teeth. She forced herself to smile, to act motherly and helpful so the twins wouldn't be scared of her.

"It's okay, it's me," she whispered. "I'm your mommy's sister, remember?"

"Mommy, Mommy," Kitty said, her eyes searching over Cory's shoulder.

Puppy began singing again. "When you wake, you will have all the pretty little horsies . . ."

"Are you guys okay? Have the Keepers been here? Did they feed you? Who knocked all those leashes down?" As Cory talked, she scanned their faces and bodies carefully. She couldn't find blood or bruises or anything like that.

The twins wouldn't look at her. Cory snaked one of her fingers through the bars of the cage and wiggled it around. "I'm here to get you out. Okay? I have to bust this lock open—it might take a minute."

"Bad Guy," Kitty said.

Cory gripped the bars so tight that her knuckles turned white. Fear coursed through her veins, but she tried to keep her voice cheerful and steady as she said, "Bad guy—what bad guy, honey? Was it Deuteronomy

29:28? The guy wearing a white and gold robe? Or was it . . . was it . . . another guy, with dark hair and a—"

"Angerman," Kitty said.

Cory started. So Angerman had been here. Had Ruth 2:10 or one of the others sent him to check on the twins? she wondered. "Angerman's a bad guy, that's right," she said out loud. "He's bad and Mommy's bad and Teacher's bad and Hunter's bad. That's why I've got to get you out of here."

The twins blinked at her. Cory saw Puppy's arm slip around Kitty's waist, and they held each other tight. Puppy began barking.

"Shhhhhh, it's okay. You have to stop that, honey, or they'll find us. I promise, this'll just take a second."

But Puppy wouldn't stop. Kitty began meowing, too. The padlock was rusty, and left a moist brownish-red mark on her skin. She raised the metal tool to it and began chiseling at it with the sharp point. She had to work fast.

The lock wouldn't give. Cory bit her lip and turned the tool in her hand to try another angle.

Puppy and Kitty continued to bark and meow. They looked more terrified than ever. "Please stop that," Cory whispered. "Please stop, or they're going to find us—don't you see that? Here, how 'bout a song? You like that pretty horsies song? Your mommy used to sing that to me when I was little—did she used to sing it to you, too?"

Still chiseling away at the padlock, Cory began singing: "When you wake, you will have all the pretty little horses. Blacks and bays, dapples and grays, all the pretty little horses. . . ."

Click. Cory felt the lock give in her hand. She tugged at it, and it pulled away from the bars and fell to the floor. Relief and pleasure washed over her—and pride, which was a feeling she hadn't known in a very long time.

Smiling, she opened the door of the cage. The twins stared at her and scrunched back even deeper into the shadows and sawdust. Cory's smile disappeared.

"No, no, it's okay," she whispered. "You guys have to come with me. This is what your mommy would have wanted. She wouldn't have wanted you to get tested, don't you see that?"

"Mommy," Puppy said.

"Yes, that's right, your mommy—"

"Let them go, Cory!"

Cory whirled around. Mommy was standing about six feet away, next to the scratching post display. Cory hadn't heard her come in; she had been so busy with the padlock and remembering about Ingrid and everything. She noticed that Mommy had a dog leash in her hand. It was one of the heavy chain ones.

Cory gulped and tried to think. What should she do now? Mommy was one of them—she was dangerous. Cory couldn't let her know that she was trying to get Puppy and Kitty out of the Crossroads.

She rose to her feet. "Ruth 2:10 ordered me to do this. It's official business—" she began.

"Let them go, get away from them!" Mommy cried out. Even in the dim light, Cory could see that the other girl's face was white with fury.

Mommy raised the chain leash in the air and took a step toward Cory. She began whipping the chain around.

"Get away from them now, or I'll *kill* you, do you understand?" she shouted.

"No, no, no!" Cory raised a hand to her face. "You don't understand, you don't understand what they're doing to you—"

Whack! Cory felt the stinging blow to the side of her head and the chain whipped around her throat. She moaned and crumpled to her knees. Dizziness overtook her like a wave.

Through the pain she felt Mommy wrap a leather leash around her wrists and tie it behind her back. Hot tears filled Cory's eyes and spilled down her cheeks. "No, you don't understand, Mommy, please, you don't understand—"

Mommy didn't reply. She unwrapped the brand-new pink scarf she was wearing around her neck, and shoved it into Cory's mouth. Cory choked and gagged, but the scarf stayed in place.

"Come on, Puppy, come on, Kitty, it's all right, Mommy's here," she heard Mommy calling out.

The twins, Ingrid's babies, scurried out of their filthy cage and went running up to Mommy. Mommy scooped them up in her arms, and without a backward glance she rushed out of the pet store.

Cory sat alone in the dark, tears coursing down her cheeks. Ingrid's babies were doomed. She had failed in her path.

Angerman tried to be helpful, carrying bikes out the fire door and gathering supplies with Hunter and Teacher. But Bad Guy wouldn't let him. Even though he was down to just a head and a torso, he was somehow making himself heavy as stone in Angerman's backpack. And he kept whispering things that made Angerman's head spin and hurt, made the rage boil up inside him so that he wanted to scream and smash things. The dog leash Angerman had wound around Bad Guy's neck wasn't doing any good.

Angerman clenched his teeth and walked over to a row of mountain bikes. Nearby, Baby and Doll and Teddy Bear were on the floor, piling water bottles and bungee cords onto a brightly painted skateboard. Action Figure was slumped against the pedestal of a skateboarding mannequin, his eyes fluttering open and shut as he watched the other kids playing. He didn't look too good.

"It is time to leave for Pis-gah," Baby announced, rolling the skateboard back and forth as if it were a toy car.

Doll held up her doll. "Dolly says she wants to take the test, too."

"Teacher knows about tests—she does 'em all the time in School," Teddy Bear said, his gaze following his sister as she lugged a silver boy's bike out the door.

"No tests today, kiddies," Angerman called out in a bright voice. "We're on vacation!"

It's not nice to lie to children, Bad Guy whispered. *Why don't you tell them the truth?*

"Shuddup."

The children stared up at him. Angerman made himself smile Real Normal and picked up a mountain bike. It had an enormous red bow tied around it with a white tag attached: PRICE REDUCED FOR CHRISTMAS! The bow was held fast to the bike with tiny wires, like tentacles. Angerman tried to untie it, but one of the wires pricked his hand, and he cursed under his breath.

Dontcha just love Christmas? Bad Guy cackled.

"I said shut up, you pathetic loser—didn't you hear me?"

"Angerman, hurry up," Hunter called out. His body was wedged in the opening of the fire door, and he was holding a purple bike with a child seat attached to the back of it. "We haven't got much time."

"Yeah, no problem."

Just then, Mommy came rushing into the bike shop. She had Puppy and Kitty in her arms. At the sight of their dirty little tearstained faces, Angerman felt his heart constrict with joy and relief.

Puppy and Kitty's frightened eyes went straight to him. He smiled and went running up to them and Mommy. "Hey, guys! Hi!"

Chestnuts roasting on an open fiiiiiire, Bad Guy sang.

Stifling a curse, Angerman reached behind his neck. His fingers found the dog leash, and he yanked on it, hard.

Owwwwww! Bad Guy complained. *Where's your Christmas spirit, boy?*

"They're okay," Mommy gasped. "That Cory girl had them. But I—I took care of her."

"Mommy! Puppy! Kitty!" Teacher came up to them. "Thank goodness, now we're all here. The bikes are all ready—let's get out of here!"

Fat chance. Bad Guy cackled. *Let's see, there's ten of*

you, and there's how many of them?

Angerman turned to Mommy and Teacher. "You guys go ahead. I'll be right back." He started sprinting toward the atrium.

"Angerman, where are you going?" he heard Mommy call out.

"I'm gonna make sure the Keepers can't follow us. Get the kids on the bikes, I'll catch up with you!"

Angerman ran, glancing this way and that to make sure there were no creepy Keepers around. The hall was deserted. He soon reached the Santa's Workshop display.

I saw Mommy kissing Saaaaanta Claus! Bad Guy sang.

Angerman's head was spinning. His backpack felt as if it weighed a thousand pounds. He realized that his fists were clenched so tightly that his nails were digging into his palms, making them bleed. He loosened his fingers and licked the blood off his palms. Muttering to himself, he reached into the pocket of his jeans, where he'd stashed a book of matches from Wix 'n' Stix the Place for Candles.

Oh, the weather outside is frightful, but the fire is so delightful! Bad Guy laughed. He began dancing and thrashing inside Angerman's backpack.

Angerman flicked the match across the matchbook. A flame crackled to life. He dropped it on top of one of the elves. The flame caught, and after a minute, the elf's entire head was on fire.

Angerman lit another match, then another and another. The air filled with a horrible black, burning smell. Soon, a roaring blaze was spreading across the fake snow-covered ground. In another minute, it would reach Santa himself.

Look at Old Nick about to get bar-bee-qued! Bad Guy cried out.

Angerman watched, mesmerized. But then he remembered that he had to get back to Mommy and the others.

His hands were streaked with blood and ashes and sweat. He rubbed them together and stuffed them into his pockets and glanced one last time at Santa Claus, who was going up in flames. Through the fire, Angerman could see Saint Nick's plastic red mouth melting into a monstrous, gaping howl.

Angerman shivered and began heading back in the direction of the bike shop. Then he stopped in his tracks and reached for his backpack. It would be so easy, throwing the entire thing into the roaring inferno . . .

Don't even think about it, boy, Bad Guy warned.

Angerman's hands stopped in midair.

Might as well throw yourself into the fire, Bad Guy hissed.

Angerman bit back a cry and shook his head so hard that it felt as if it would break off. Then he began running down the hall.

Chapter Eleven

Mommy's hands were still shaking with rage and fear as she snapped the chin strap of Baby's safety helmet into place. "Get on your bike, Baby, hurry up."

"Where's Angerman?" Hunter asked, squeezing his brake handles with white-knuckled fists. On the back of his bike, Puppy sat crammed into the baby seat and blinking in the bright sunlight. "What's taking him so long?"

"Teacher, get started with the kids," Mommy begged. She looked over her shoulder, where the silver-gray bicycle stood propped against the building. A thin trail of smoke from somewhere in the center of the mall rose above the roof and disappeared into the white heat of the daylight. Was that the bonfire on the other side of the Crossroads? Where the Keepers were waiting for them to come back and burn their precious Book. That was jammed inside Angerman's backpack . . . She gulped. "Teacher, go! Go on ahead, we'll catch up."

"Aren't we waiting for Angerman?" Teddy Bear asked.

Teacher shifted the loaded backpack strapped to her shoulders and shook her head. "No. We're going to get a head start. Let's go!"

"Follow signs for the Interstate going north!" Hunter called as Teacher led the children away.

Doll looked back, and Mommy gave her a brave

smile. "Go with Teacher. Let me see how fast you can ride!"

Mommy watched for a second, watched the kids wobbling and swerving across the weed-grown pavement behind Teacher. Action Figure wobbled quite a bit, and Mommy squelched a pang of worry. She couldn't think about Action Figure right now: they had to get away, get away as fast as possible. When they were safe, then they could see what was wrong with him, why he was so tired. She turned around and hoisted Kitty up into the seat on the back of her own bike, then strapped the little girl in. She could feel Kitty's eyes on her, on her hands fumbling with the straps. What could this little girl possibly make of what she had seen Mommy do to Cory? Did she understand what had happened? Mommy wasn't sure herself, for that matter, didn't know how that powerful wave of fury and vengeance had moved her arm, her hands, brought shouts of rage from her throat, whipped that girl with the— And how it wrapped like a snake around her throat, and that horrible choking sound. What if Cory died? What if—

The delivery door to X-treme Byxx slammed open and clanged back against the stucco, sending chips flying as Angerman burst outside. He grabbed the silver bike, hauled it around, and kicked off, swinging his leg up and over. He shot toward Mommy and Hunter, with Bad Guy lurching from side to side in the backpack as he pumped the pedals.

"Let's get out of here!" he shouted. The wind swooshed Mommy's hair back as Angerman swept by.

Hunter and Mommy stood on their pedals. A strong wind bowed the palm trees and rattled the fronds, and an old scrap of newspaper dipped and swooped in the air. VACATION AT THE BEACH! cried the advertising headline in faded capitals. Kitty struggled in the seat, throwing Mommy off balance.

"Hang on, Kitty," Mommy yelled. "We're going far, far away!"

They could see Teacher and the others ahead, coasting down the ramp to the arterial that linked the mall to the highway. Empty cars, trucks, and buses were halted here and there, some smashed into each other and rusting together like fallen trees rotting into one mass of decay on the forest floor. Mommy concentrated on zigzagging around the derelicts and avoiding puddles. A trio of pelicans sat on an overpass, blinking down at the group of bicycles whizzing by beneath. Mommy felt the cool splash of shade as she rode through, and then the slam of hot sun again as she shot out the other side. Mommy leaned into the wind and caught up to Action Figure. She glanced his way as she came alongside. A deep frown creased his forehead, and he gripped his handlebars as if hanging on for dear life.

"Come on, Action, why aren't you up there beating the girls?" Mommy joshed him, but she didn't think she sounded very convincing. He didn't answer, didn't even look her way, just pedaled doggedly with his eyes on the road just ahead of his front wheel.

"That's good, just keep it going," Mommy said.

"Interstate's ahead!" Hunter's voice reached back to them.

"Come on, Action!" Mommy called, pedaling harder and pulling ahead.

Up in front she saw them—her *family*, not phony

Brothers and Sisters—all zoom left across the road beneath a dead traffic light and up another ramp. One, two, three, four—the little girls on their bikes, Teacher and Hunter and Teddy Bear, and Angerman leaning over the handlebars with Bad Guy leering over his shoulder. Mommy felt a surge of joy and relief to be moving, away from the strange and sticky spiderweb the Keepers had spun around them all. Ahead of her she saw Puppy clinging to Hunter's shirt, and her heart swelled with love. She had saved them. She didn't know exactly what she had saved them from, but she knew it was bad and knew that whatever she had done to Cory, she was justified.

Unless she had killed her. Then what did that make her? Mommy squeezed her eyes shut to blot out the image of Cory falling to the floor of the pet shop. When she opened them again, she was soaring up onto an overpass with Kitty's thin arms wrapped tightly around her waist. Behind her to the left, she saw the vast bulk of the Crossroads sitting in its wasteland of parking lot. A plume of black smoke was boiling up from the mall. She could see it clearly, pouring through one of the skylights of the atrium.

"That's not the bonfire!" she gasped. "Hey! The Crossroads is on fire!"

Angerman let out a wild shout of triumph. "Can a man take fire in his bosom and his clothes not be *BURNED*? NOOOOOOOOO!"

Angerman's howl trailed after them as they raced up the interstate, with Action Figure falling farther and farther behind.

* * *

They had been riding for a long time, long enough for the sun to shift past the zenith, and the heat throbbed like a heartbeat. Teacher could feel her shirt sticking to her skin underneath the backpack, and she could see by the looks of exhaustion on everyone else's face that they had to rest. She glanced over her shoulder, as much as she could without the pack throwing her off balance. Action Figure was so far back he was almost lost to view. Teacher gripped hard on the brake handles and almost fell.

"Hunter!" she cried out. "Stop!"

Tires whined under brake clamps. Baby and Doll let their bikes stop, and they each hopped off to flop in the weeds at the side of the road. Hunter circled back, and came abreast of Teacher.

"Take Puppy," he said, his eyes on his little brother. "Get him off my bike!"

Teacher let her own bike fall to the ground as she stepped off, then grabbed Puppy under the armpits. "Woopsy-daisy," she said, and gulped down a laugh at the ridiculous phrase that came from someplace deep in her memory.

Unburdened, Hunter raced back to Action Figure, his bike tipping side to side to side with the force of his pedaling. The others stood astride their bikes or sat on the grassy edge of the highway. Teacher unclipped the buckle of her waist strap and let the heavy pack slide to the ground. Teddy Bear was lying down on top of his pack, like an overturned turtle.

"What is wrong with Action?" Mommy said, lifting Kitty out of her seat.

"I don't know," Teacher said. "I know he's been pretty quiet lately—do you think he's sick?"

"He's never sick," Mommy said. "He's just—tired."

Angerman pulled a pack of matches out of his pocket and fingered them with a faraway look on his face. "What are the chances he had all his vaccinations before Fire-us? He could have anything—monks, weasels, chicken pots—"

"Be quiet, Angerman," Teacher said. She and Mommy stood in the road, catching their breath and watching as Hunter joined his brother. They watched him take Action Figure's red knapsack off him and put it over his own shoulders. He seemed to be urging his brother along, but even from a distance it was clear the kid was near the end of his strength.

"We need to find a place to rest." Mommy's voice was firm.

"We're not all that far away from the Crossroads," Angerman said, shaking his head. He ripped out a match and struck it, the flame almost invisible in the bright sunshine. "I don't know, seems to me—"

"So what are you trying to say?" Mommy turned on him. "So we just leave Action behind? What choice do we have?"

Teacher looked around, letting her gaze rest briefly on Teddy Bear, on Baby and Doll lying in the grass, on Puppy and Kitty who squatted on their haunches poking at an enormous dead beetle. Not far up the road was an overturned tractor-trailer, jackknifed across one lane. The cab was belly-up in the middle of the highway, and the trailer itself angled down into a ditch. Its doors gaped open facing the tangle of palmetto scrub at the side of the highway, and a stream of trash—it looked like dozens and dozens of shoes—was scattered behind it as if the doors had burst open in the crash. Ants and maggots worked busily at a mouse carcass near where Teacher stood. She stooped and flicked the body away by the tail.

"There, we can rest in there." She pointed at the trailer.

Mommy turned around and a smile broke across her face. "Excellent. But—" Her smile vanished, and she lowered her voice. "We have to check it out first for bones and wild animals without letting the kids know we're doing it."

"I'll go." Angerman scraped another match into flame, and then shook it out. "I'll do it."

Angerman rode ahead to investigate, while Mommy went to distract the little ones. Teacher opened the backpack, hoping to find granola bars or some bottles of water—anything to revive them all—but it seemed to be all freeze-dried food, nothing they could eat dry without choking. The whirring of cicadas throbbed against her eardrums, making the heat more intense. She looked up as Action Figure came toiling up, with Hunter riding alongside. Action Figure's bleached white hair was ropy with sweat, and even though the sun was fierce, he was pale.

"Wanna stop," he mumbled.

"We're going to— Hunter, catch him!"

Before Hunter could move, Action Figure had toppled to the ground. Teacher and Hunter both lunged for him. A cut on his cheek bled scarlet against his ashen face. Hunter gathered his little brother up in his arms.

"There, the trailer," Teacher said, pointing ahead.

Angerman was standing in the opening of the trailer, waving them all on.

"Come on, kids!" Teacher clapped her hands. "Get on your bikes again. You just have to ride to that big truck there where Angerman is. Come on. Hurry up! Puppy and Kitty, come on—you can walk the rest of the way."

Grumbling and whining, the younger children pushed their bicycles up the road behind Mommy. Teacher swung the pack over her shoulders. It felt so much heavier than it had before that she let out a small groan, and as she leaned over to pick up her bike the pack banged into the back of her head. Teacher swung her arms, trying to regain her balance, surprised at how tired she was.

"Put all the bikes inside," Angerman was saying as she reached the trailer. "All the way inside. Lots of room."

"It's hot in here!" Doll complained.

"Just do it," Angerman said. "Come on, hurry up."

Their footsteps thunked and echoed inside the big metal box, and Mommy began shoving cartons of sneakers aside to make room, and she scraped away a big spiderweb with a piece of cardboard.

Teacher saw Angerman scanning the road behind them. She paused and looked back, too. Waves of heat shimmered and wobbled over the baking path of asphalt, and mirages like broad puddles stretched from edge to edge.

"Did you see something?" she asked in an undertone.

Angerman shrugged. "I'm not sure."

Teacher regarded him for a moment. He might be crazy, but he wasn't stupid, and he definitely had moments of complete sanity. A flicker of alarm went through Teacher, and she turned to the others. The young children were pawing through the contents of the trailer, boxes full of athletic shoes, their voices loud with protest and crankiness. Hunter was settling Action Figure on a pallet of cardboard way in the deepest end of the steel trailer, and Mommy was hovering over him, too. The entryway was cluttered with bicycles and bright white, newly spilled sneakers. They were so white they almost seemed to shine.

"Okay, let's go, in, in, in," she said in her most teacherly way. "Bikes, bring your bikes in."

Angerman stood at the entry, eyes fixed on the heat shimmer and mirages while the rest of them bustled their bikes and gear inside, out of view. He stood like a sentinel, silhouetted against the bright glare, with Bad Guy's head at his shoulder. A gecko scurried up the edge of the open door. Teacher shooed the children farther inside. "Action is sleeping, so we have to be very quiet," she said. "No noise."

Then she heard it. She whirled around and saw Angerman pull back suddenly from the brightness into the shadow. There were hoofbeats, and the rattle of wheels on pavement. Teacher saw Mommy's eyes gleam in the shadows as they widened. She put her finger to her lips.

"I'm thirsty," Teddy Bear said.

"Shhh!" Mommy put her arm across his shoulders. "Just for a minute," she whispered.

The clatter was louder, nearer. Teacher felt her pulse beat in time with the pounding of hooves. Back at the Crossroads she had seen only four chariots altogether. Just four. Two had gone south, according to Teddy Bear. Looking for Ingrid, or was that a coincidence? And one had gone to someplace called Pisgah, according to Baby and Doll. So there could only be one chariot left, one horse. The hollow steel box of the trailer captured the sound and amplified it until it seemed as if the chariot were about to drive right inside and trample them all. Teacher felt herself bracing for impact.

Then the sound rattled past and faded. Angerman stepped outside and peeked around the door.

"I have to go pee," Doll whispered.

"In a minute, honey," Mommy said. "Just wait another minute."

They all watched Angerman. After a long moment, he came back into the hot darkness and sat beside Teacher. "The red horse. One Keeper. Kept going."

Mommy crouched down beside Angerman and Teacher. "What should we do? Do you think they're looking for us?"

"Oh, gosh, no, you think so?" Angerman said in a fake-dimwit voice. "Why would they look for *us*? It's just a total coincidence."

Teacher jabbed him with her elbow. "All right, all right—they're looking for us. For now we need to stay here anyway, 'cause of Action."

"But then?" Mommy's voice rose. "We have to keep going! We can't just stay here."

In that moment, Teacher remembered the maps that

Teddy Bear had found for her. "Where's The Book? Angerman, do you have it?" she asked as she unzipped her fanny pack and drew out the brittle, blackened pages.

While Angerman dug in his backpack, Hunter joined them, holding out two water bottles. "He's asleep. I guess he's sick. I'm gonna have to get some medicine."

Teacher took The Book from Angerman and opened it, tipping it toward the light. The stiff, collaged pages popped and crackled as she let them riffle past her thumb. When the pages stopped moving on their own, she flattened The Book and spread out one of the burned maps across it. At the top of the map, a red winged horse leaped through the air. "I think we really should stick to the highway and keep going north," she mused, squinting at the scorched map fragments. She reached for a bottle and took a slug of water. "It's the straightest way. There's a city called . . . Savan—*Savannah*. We should head for that."

"But what about the chariot guy, that Keeper who just went by?" Mommy said. "What if he comes back and we bump right into him?"

"Besides, there's nothing to hunt on the highway," Hunter pointed out.

Angerman made a snorting sound. "Look, we had this argument before. We stick to the highway, or else we'll get lost. This highway goes to Washington, and that's where we'll find President."

"But I have to get something for Action!" Hunter argued, his voice rising. "He's sick!"

"And I'm tired of being an orphan and living like an

animal!" Angerman snapped. "The world is totally messed up, there's a bunch of freaky religious wackos looking for us, and we're all neck deep in serious doo-doo, Hunter. What else is new?"

"Stop it, stop it!" Mommy said. "That's enough! We all have to figure this out together."

The boys glared at each other, not speaking. In the silence, Kitty let out a frightened mew, and then they all heard it: the sound of hoofbeats returning. Angerman darted to the entrance to spy around the corner, and Teacher tightened her grip on The Book, the one link they had to the Before Time. This time, if the Keepers tried to take it from her, she would kill to protect it.

But once again, the chariot rattled past and the sound faded, dying out toward the south. In the darkness of the trailer, Teacher felt a bead of sweat trickle down her back, and the sharp smell of pee reached her from where the little ones were.

Had the Keeper given up the search? Or was he going back for reinforcements?

The heat lingered even after the sun went down. The western sky glowed orange and red, and in the east the sky was dark enough to show a star or two. Angerman stood in the weeds outside the trailer, facing east, where the highway curved around a swamp. Dead pines rose from the mud like fingers pointing to the sky. The ocean was not far away, he knew that, could smell it and feel it in the air. Once, there had been a time when you could stand on the beach and see lights out there in the darkness, cargo ships going places, sailboats with their canvas sails belled out over the whispering waves, big white power yachts with people drinking cocktails and listening to jazz and flirting with each other, talking politics. Angerman couldn't remember if he had ever seen that himself, standing on a beach in the dark and seeing the lights. He thought he had. Maybe he had.

Or maybe you're just making it up, Bad Guy suggested. *Maybe you just saw it on the tee-veeeee.*

"I did see it," Angerman muttered. "Just leave me alone."

And sometimes, walking in the wet sand where the tide was just washing over, there were tiny glowing animals that lit up when you kicked the water, making the waves visible in the dark, like a sudden burst of stars.

That's a bunch of baloney.

"No, it's true, it's true," Angerman said through gritted teeth. He could feel tears coming.

What are you so afraid of, huh? Not a little red horsey? A weetle wed horsey-worsey?

"No, no," Angerman said. He paced, and kicked his feet through the weeds, but there was no glow of starlight. "One times one is one, one times two is—"

Oh, puh-leeez. Repeat after me: 'And there went out another horse . . .'

"'And there went out another horse that was red,'" Angerman said as tears welled up in his eyes.

Thaaaaat's right.

"'And power was given to him that sat thereon'—no, I don't want to—"

"Power was given to him." Go on!

"'And power was given to him that sat thereon,'" Angerman babbled. "'And peace to the heart, and love of one another: and there was given to him—'"

Yeeeeeesssss?

"'And there was given to him a great sword.'"

Bad Guy smiled in the darkness. *That's right. Good boy.*

Chapter Twelve

Hunter woke up to pitch darkness, his muscles stiff and aching, his face drenched with sweat. He didn't know where he was, and he couldn't make himself wake up enough to figure it out. His brain was still in the fog of his dream: something about a baby, something about a horse, lots of confusion and noise and shouting. He reached up to touch his face and realized that the wetness wasn't sweat. It was tears.

Hunter swiped at his eyes and sat up. A gray-black cloud moved across the sky, and the room was suddenly bright. He glanced around. No, he wasn't in a room; he was in the tractor-trailer. Moonlight was flooding in through the open cargo doors, along with a cool breeze that smelled like beach and the soft, steady hum of crickets. *Finest accommodations in Jacksonville, convenient to the highway and all stores and restaurants.* He tried to laugh at his joke, but somehow, he didn't feel like laughing.

Something warm brushed against his side. He glanced down and realized with a start that Teacher was sleeping next to him. She never did this; it wasn't like her at all. She usually slept with Mommy and the girls, or with Teddy Bear.

Then Hunter saw that Teacher's body was curled around The Book. In the moonlight, he could see that her forehead was creased with worry and that her lips were moving, making silent nonsense words. The Book was open to somewhere in the middle. The fingers of her right hand were spread across the open pages, over a Magic Marker with no cap on it.

Hunter leaned toward Teacher and The Book, full of curiosity. He knew that The Book was sacred and that only Teacher was supposed to look at it, technically speaking. He couldn't help but wonder, though: What had she been recording? Did it have something to do with him? Teacher often listened to the children's sleep babbles and wrote them down. Or the entries would simply appear in The Book, and Teacher would discover them the next morning and recite them to everyone during School. Either way, they were part of the family's history.

Teacher's hand was in Hunter's way. He reached over and nudged it slowly, slowly off the page. He kept his gaze fixed on Teacher the whole time. He could feel his heart hammering in his chest.

"By the Flame," Teacher whispered. From outside, an owl hooted.

Hunter froze and stared at her. Her eyes were closed.

"Teacher?" Hunter whispered. "You awake?"

Teacher didn't reply. She lifted her hand to her face, as if to shield it from something. And then she rolled away from him, away from The Book, and curled up into a tight ball. And lay very still.

He stared at her for a second longer. He could see her bony shoulder blades moving up and down under her T-shirt. When he realized that she was asleep, he inched his body closer to The Book. He didn't have his glasses on, so he had to squint.

The Book was open to one of the burned map

fragments Teddy Bear had found in the Crossroads parking lot. There was a picture of a red horse on the top of it, its body arced as if it were flying through the air, and its wings were stretched out behind it. There were words scrawled across northern Florida and part of the Atlantic Ocean, in Teacher's handwriting:

MOMMY AND DADDY AREN'T HERE
STOP CRYING
STOP CRYING I'LL FIX YOUR
ROCKING HORSE FOR YOU

Hunter felt his body go cold. His dream—that was his dream. He had been dreaming about a baby crying. The baby had been crying for his mom and dad, crying for them to fix the broken handle on his rocking horse so he could ride it again.

Except, the dream had really happened. It had happened five years ago, just after Fire-us.

Hunter pushed The Book away and scrambled to his feet. Pain shot through his calves from the long hard bike ride, and he wobbled for a second. Across the trailer, he could just make out the blurry outline of Action Figure curled up on the floor. He stepped over a bunch of sleeping bodies—Mommy, Doll, Baby, and Teddy Bear—then knelt down beside his little brother.

Action Figure was hardly moving. His face was ashy-pale—almost gray—and his hair was matted with sweat. Hunter touched the back of his hand to the boy's forehead, just like he'd seen Mommy do so many times. It seemed way hotter than it should be, even with the heat and all.

Hunter swore under his breath. He called himself Hunter—the hunter for the family, the provider—but what had he provided for Action Figure lately? He had been so obsessed with fitting in with the Brothers that he had totally ignored his one, true brother. And while he was hanging out with the Brothers and harnessing the horses and acting all manly, Action Figure had gotten sick.

Now they were stuck in this hot, cramped tractor-trailer, with no medicine and not nearly enough food and water. There was no way Action Figure would be able to continue riding his bike in the morning. And who could say when that Keeper would return with his red horse and chariot?

Hunter started. The red horse. Yes, that was it, he had to get the red horse!

It all made sense. The red-horse symbol in Teacher's Book. His memory-dream about fixing the rocking horse for Action Figure. If only Hunter could go back to the Crossroads Mall and steal the red horse and chariot, they could continue the journey north more easily—he on the red horse, Action Figure in the chariot. Action Figure would get better, and before long would be able to ride the red horse himself. Hunter remembered how Action Figure had taken to the red horse that first day, when they had run into Ruth 2:10 on the beach. The red horse would help Action Figure.

And stealing the red horse would serve another purpose, too. As far as Hunter and the rest of the family knew, there were only four horses and chariots at the Crossroads. And three of those horses and chariots had gone on long, faraway trips, which meant that if Hunter took the last horse and chariot, it would make it all the harder for the Keepers to follow them north to Savannah.

Hunter cast one last glance at Action Figure and brushed a lock of damp hair from his forehead. "Hang in there, kiddo," he whispered. "I'm gonna get you a rocking horse." Then he rose to his feet and headed outside, grabbing his backpack as he went.

Cory stumbled through the dark hall toward Entrance East, her breath coming in ragged gasps. Her wedding dress kept tangling up in her ankles, and the shoes were impossible: pinchy toes and tall, pointy heels that made her wobble. But the Keepers had taken all her other clothes and shoes away from her, and she didn't dare risk stopping at the Gap or Banana Republic to shop for a new outfit. She knew they were posting guards all over the mall, after what had happened today.

What *had* happened today? Her eyes stung with fresh tears at the thought of Ingrid's children being whisked away by that insane girl Mommy.

Mommy had left Cory at the pet shop for dead after attacking her with the dog chain. But where did Mommy and her friends go after that? Cory had lain there on the floor of the pet shop, crying and dizzy with pain, until the Keeper women had found her there. They asked her a lot of questions, and there was a lot of whispering among them. From what she'd overheard, it sounded as if Mommy and the others had set fire to the mall and then escaped to who knows where on bikes. The fire had destroyed about half the mall, leaving only the east and west wings intact. The north wing was totally gutted and unlivable, and the south wing was almost as bad. Even now, the air was heavy with the black, acrid smell of smoke.

None of this made sense. Why hadn't Mommy delivered Puppy and Kitty to the Keepers? Where were they now?

Cory touched the side of her face, which was puffy and tender and painful from where Mommy had whacked it with the chain. It was sticky, too—whether with blood or the concealer makeup the Keeper women had smeared all over it, she wasn't sure. And her throat felt bruised from the leash whipping around her neck.

"The schedule has been escalated," Ruth 2:10 had said to her after an emergency meeting at the Cine-Theater. "The women will take you to Danielle's Bridal Shoppe to get you into your special clothes. You will be sent away to Pisgah first thing in the morning. Isn't that wonderful news?"

In the firelit darkness, the Keepers had begun chanting: "'Let us be glad and rejoice, and give honor to him: for the marriage of the Lamb is come, and his wife hath made herself ready.'"

Cory slowed her steps. Her feet hurt, her head hurt, and, besides, it was difficult to see in the pitch-black. It was a cloudy night, so the moonlight shining through the skylights was sporadic, undependable. She had decided not to use a flashlight or lantern or candle, because she didn't want to make herself any more conspicuous than necessary. Besides, her white veil kept falling over her eyes, and she had to swat it aside in impatience.

"'And Jesus answering said unto them, The children of this world marry, and are given in marriage.'"

She could smell the horse now, its sweat and manure. She realized that she must be near the loading dock. She reached out her left hand and touched the cool tile wall so that she could follow it to the exit.

"'Again, he sent forth other servants, saying, Tell them which are bidden, Behold, I have prepared my dinner: my oxen and my fatlings are killed, and all things are ready: come unto the marriage.'"

Cory stumbled ahead in the darkness. Wall, wall, wall . . . and then it curved around, and then she was touching glass and metal.

She pressed her face against the pane. She could hear the horse's gentle whinnying noises, strange for this time of night when it should be sleeping. It seemed to be excited about something—perhaps the terror of the fire still making it uneasy, or maybe an armadillo had bumbled into it in the dark. Because of the angle of the door, she couldn't see the horse or the chariot. She could just barely make out one side of the loading dock, a couple of broken wooden pallets, a pile of hay. And a bike. Cory sucked in her breath in surprise.

She gathered her rustling white skirt in her hands and opened the door. She should be able to harness the horse; she had watched the Keeper men do it a hundred times. The question was, would she be able to do it quickly and then get away, before any of the Keepers discovered that she was missing from her bed?

And *then* what? She had to find Puppy and Kitty. She had no idea how she was going to find them in all of Jacksonville or wherever Mommy had taken them. But she *had* to find them, for Ingrid's sake. She had failed in her path once; she wasn't going to fail again.

She stepped over the body of a dead seagull and rushed over to where the chariot was parked, just beyond the loading dock. The red horse was next to it, pawing in agitation at the asphalt pavement.

"What's the matter, boy?" she called out in a soft voice.

The horse lifted its nose in the air and then looked right at her, snorting. A figure stepped out from behind it. "Stop right there!"

Cory froze in her tracks. With trembling fingers, she lifted her veil over her head, to see. It wasn't one of the Keepers. It was the Hunter boy. He had the horse's leather bridle in his hands.

Cory stared at him in shock. "Wh-what are you doing here?"

Hunter pushed his glasses up his nose and stared back at her. "I could ask you the same question. What's up with the outfit? Isn't that a wedding dress?"

"Yes."

Cory didn't bother to explain further. Her mind was racing. What was Hunter doing here? Where were Mommy and Teacher and Angry Man and the others? Obviously, Hunter was stealing the horse and chariot to take back to them. But *she* needed the horse and chariot to get away, too.

But Hunter must know where Ingrid's children were.

There was only one way to handle this, as far as she could see. She took a step toward Hunter, lifted her chin, and looked at him square in the eyes. "Take me with you," she demanded.

Hunter shook his head. "No way."

"Take me with you," Cory repeated, more loudly this time. "You take me or I'll . . . I'll scream. That's right, I'll scream!"

Hunter opened his mouth and then clamped it shut. He seemed to be considering something.

He glanced over Cory's shoulder at the mall entrance. "I don't get it," he said. "Aren't you one of them?"

"No. Are you?"

Hunter laughed a harsh, dry-sounding laugh. "Yeah, right." His eyeglasses caught a faint gleam of moonlight as he turned toward her. "Okay. You can come. Help me get this horse ready, will you?"

Cory tried not to sound too relieved. "Sure."

Hunter worked the bridle over the horse's head, and then the two of them got to work on the harness, feeling their way in the darkness. The only sounds in the air were the clanking of metal buckles and the horse's quiet snorts.

"Are . . . are Puppy and Kitty okay?" Cory said after a minute.

Hunter's voice sounded surprised. "They're fine. Why are you—"

But Cory didn't hear any more. Something had caught her attention. Inside Entrance East, two pinpricks of light were bobbing and weaving in the dark hallway. They were getting larger and larger.

"Hunter!" she whispered, grabbing his arm. "Over there! There's someone coming!"

Hunter whirled around. "Oh, great," he muttered.

"Come on—we've gotta go!"

Hunter checked the harness one last time, then hitched his backpack over his shoulders and hoisted himself into the chariot. He held out a hand to help her up, but she ignored it. She bunched the skirt of her wedding dress in her hands and climbed on board. One of her white shoes caught on the edge of the chariot and fell onto the pavement.

"No time to get that!" Hunter growled, grabbing the leather reins. "Let's go!"

Just as the chariot pulled away from the loading dock, two of the Keeper men came bursting out of Entrance East, carrying spears. Cory recognized them as Jeremiah 7:19 and Amos 8:10.

"Halt!" Jeremiah 7:19 cried out. "In the name of the Supreme Leader, halt and return to your brethren!"

Amos 8:10 held up his spear. "By the Flame!"

On an impulse, Cory took off her other white shoe and flung it at the two men. It caught Amos 8:10 on the forehead, and he stumbled backward. Jeremiah 7:19 grabbed him to keep him from falling, then turned and shouted something at Cory. But she couldn't hear him above the horse's hoofbeats.

"What are you *doing*?" Hunter hissed at her.

"'The fire consumed their young men; and their maidens were *not* given in marriage,'" Cory replied.

"*What?*"

Cory laughed. The horse broke into a gallop. The sky was still black, although there was one faint gold streak across the horizon, signaling the dawn. As Hunter guided the chariot toward I-95, Cory reached up and ripped the veil off her head and let it go flying behind her. The white gauzy fabric caught on a current and whipped around and then disappeared in the darkness, like a ghost.

Chapter Thirteen

Teacher woke early, just as the light began spreading across the horizon in the east. Pine trees stood dark and angular against the brightening sky, and as Teacher watched, a cloud of white egrets rose from their night place and flapped southward on silent wings. It was cool, and the air was moist and soft on Teacher's cheek. She lay looking out through the open trailer door, knowing the day would be hard but enjoying for a brief moment the quiet and the ease. She sighed, resting her chin on her hands.

"You awake?"

Teacher craned around at the sound of Mommy's voice. "Yeah."

Mommy crawled toward her, and they lay on their stomachs side by side, looking out. They were silent, watching the sky change from peach to apricot in long streaks. Birds called out to the day, and trails of mist wove through the tall weeds. At last, Mommy spoke.

"Hunter's not here," she said in a low voice.

"What?" Teacher sat up and looked into the depths of the trailer. The shadows were still too deep to show anything but humped, sleeping forms. As she turned around again her gaze fell on the tangle of bikes sprawled in the grass: five, six, seven—her bike was missing.

"I heard him go—but I thought I was dreaming,"

Mommy said. "I was so tired I couldn't wake up."

"Maybe he went to look for some breakfast," Teacher suggested.

Mommy looked out into the gloom. "It was still dark. It was the middle of the night."

Teacher tucked her knees up and wrapped her arms around them, rocking. What did it mean, Hunter leaving in the middle of the night? Where would he go? What if something happened to him and he couldn't get back to them? What if he ran into one of those Keepers? She squeezed her eyes shut tight, trying to keep the bad thoughts from crowding in.

Then she blinked. The Book. Of course. Consult The Book.

Relief wrapped around her heart. Teacher already felt calmer, just knowing she could turn to their own history for guidance. For as long as she could remember, since Fire-us, The Book had been their oracle, their almanac, their record of days. It gave answers when hard mysteries arose. To be sure, the answers were often unclear. But Teacher had learned to meditate on the signs and words she found there, and wait for their meaning to become clear to her. It was a heavy responsibility, but she never questioned why it had been given to her.

And to think that it had almost been destroyed—but Angerman had rescued it. Angerman. He had not even been part of their family all that long, so The Book didn't have the same special meaning to him that it had to the others, it didn't inspire the same fearful awe. But that was what saved it. Even in a crisis, neither Mommy nor

Hunter would have dreamed of touching The Book. But Angerman had snatched it out of Deuteronomy 29:28's hands and run away with it. Teacher wondered if he even realized how much he had saved.

She glanced at him as she picked her way among the sleeping children to pick up The Book. Angerman lay on his side, with Puppy and Kitty spooned on either side of him. He was so dangerous and so brave, so crazy and so kind. He was one thing Teacher had not yet tried to find answers about in The Book. She always wrote down what he said when he veered off into one of his raving speeches, because she sensed it was real Information. He knew things, even if he didn't realize it himself. Teacher had a strong feeling that in due time, the answer to the big riddle of Angerman would be revealed by The Book. Until then, she didn't want to ask it something it couldn't tell her yet.

But it could certainly tell her what to do with Hunter gone, and why. The heavy weight of it was comforting to her as Teacher stepped outside into the gathering light. She sat on a flattened cardboard box, while Mommy sat nearby in respectful silence. One by one, Teacher let the thick, pasted pages flip past her thumb. They flashed magazine pictures, words, newspaper clippings, photographs, handwriting, stickers, scraps of wrapping paper, cash register receipts, envelopes, postcards, brochures—countless pieces of printed signs and symbols of the Before Time—past her eyes. There was an entry from a year ago—no, two years ago—when lightning had split a tree in two on their street. Here was a handwritten entry from their trip up the river, about

Teddy Bear and alligators. Teacher traced her fingertip over her own handwriting. Then she let another clump of pages flip past.

The pages popped open to an advertisement for Tricorner Bookstore, a schedule of after-school programs at the Wilson Harbor Public Library, and a magazine photograph of two children sitting in their First Mommy's lap, reading a big, colorful book. Scrawled across all these in large red block letters was a sentence: "And no man in heaven, nor in earth, neither under the earth, was able to open the book, neither to look thereon."

Teacher stared at the writing. Had she written it? It did happen, sometimes, that she couldn't remember writing in The Book. Sometimes it seemed as if things just appeared on its pages by magic when it was time to see them. But whenever she found handwriting in it, whether she remembered writing it herself or not, it always seemed to belong there.

But this—what was it? The red blocky letters seemed almost to vibrate on the page. What was this message The Book was giving her? Teacher looked off into the distance, trying to settle her mind.

Was The Book telling her not to open it anymore? Neither to look thereon?

She had never seen this before, she was sure of that. The Book had been saved from the bonfire, but now it was telling her . . . not to open it? Not look at it? Teacher felt herself grow cold.

"What does it say?" Mommy whispered.

Teacher turned to Mommy with a blank face. "Uh . . . it doesn't . . ."

"What?"

"It doesn't say anything about Hunter," Teacher said, and shut the book with a snap.

Mommy left Teacher sitting on the ground, and she tiptoed inside the trailer. Deep in the shadows at the back, Action Figure was lying with his head pillowed on his knapsack. He seemed to be sleeping a more regular sleep, not the fitful, feverish unconsciousness of last night. Maybe— Could he be getting better? Mommy laid a hand on his brow and brushed the hair back from his forehead. She hadn't been able to touch Action Figure in a long time—he hadn't let her without growling, or even biting. During their last year in Lazarus he had become so wild and skittish it was as if he were reverting to some primal state. But now, lying asleep, he was just a sick little boy, and Mommy's heart ached for him. He had to get better. He had to.

"Time to rise and shine," came Angerman's voice.

Mommy turned around in time to see Angerman pull the twins around and start tickling them. They giggled and squirmed, and the noise woke up the other children who piled on for a huge tickle fight. Angerman disappeared under a mass of thin arms and legs. Shrieks and squeals of laughter drowned out his muffled squawk.

"Don't kill him!" Mommy laughed.

Action Figure stirred and opened his eyes to watch the roughhousing, but he didn't make any move to join in. Teddy Bear extracted himself from the pile and ran outside, holding his crotch, and Mommy saw Teacher pointing to a place far back in the weeds where he could pee. The tall grasses jerked and swayed as he hurried through.

"Hunna?" Action Figure's voice was weak.

Mommy leaned over him. "Hunter? He's not here, but he'll be right back," she said. "Just try to sleep. I'll wake you up when he gets here."

Then she stood and walked over to the tickle pile, where Angerman lay on his back, pinned down with Baby and Doll on his arms, Puppy on his legs, and Kitty sitting cross-legged on his chest. Angerman looked up at Mommy through the tangle of his curly hair. "They got me."

"Okay, everybody out, out, out," Mommy said, shooing the children outside. "Everybody find a place to have a pee, and then we'll have breakfast."

The sun was sitting on top of the horizon now, and because the road curved eastward around a swamp studded with dead trees, the sun seemed to be resting right out on the end of the highway. Mommy stood shielding her eyes from the glare as the kids tumbled out of the trailer and scattered. Something flickered. She squinted, half-blinded by the light. It was something nodding and bobbing, racing toward them out of the sun.

Then she knew what it was.

"Chariot!" she cried out. "Hurry, get back inside! Run!"

Screaming, the children struggled to get out of the weeds. Baby tripped, and Puppy began barking in fear. Grasshoppers leaped out ahead of them, and one clung to Kitty's hair. Teacher ran after Teddy Bear, while Angerman scooped Kitty up from behind a tuft of palmetto. "I can't find Dolly!" Doll wailed. "I dropped Dolly—where is she?!"

They could hear the clatter of wheels coming closer now. "We'll find Dolly later!" Mommy yelled. "Get inside!"

"No, no!" Doll stood in the waist-high weeds, sobbing.

Mommy bit back a cry of impatience and ran out to where the girl stood. In her terror, Doll hadn't even noticed that Dolly was tucked in the back of her waistband. "Here she is," Mommy said, plucking the doll out and handing it over. "Now scoot!"

But even as they ran, the chariot came racing out of the sun up the road. There was no hiding, now. Mommy pushed Doll down into the tall grass and flung herself on top of her.

"It's the princess!" Doll shrieked, her voice muffled.

Mommy raised her head. "What?"

She looked up as the horse broke its canter and trotted, finally coming to a halt. Hunter was at the reins, and Cory, in her wedding dress, stood beside him. Mommy felt her stomach roll over. Doll wriggled out from underneath her and began to run.

"Hunter!"

At once, everyone was clamoring and yelling, and Hunter was wrapping the horse's reins around a bar at the top of the chariot. Cory jumped down and reached back for two jugs of water. The red horse snorted, its sides heaving.

"You went back to the Crossroads?" Teacher said. "Why? How?"

"It's a long story," Hunter replied.

"You stole the chariot," Angerman said with a huge grin. "That is too excellent for words."

Mommy picked herself up off the ground, brushing the stray grass seeds that stuck to her clothes. She could feel her face prickling with heat, but whether it was anger or embarrassment or disappearing fear she couldn't say.

"What's she doing here?" she asked.

Cory had been handing out oranges, but she paused for a moment and looked at Mommy. There was a long purple bruise on the side of her face that looked puffy and sore, and there were red, raw marks on her throat. She held Mommy's gaze, and then turned to Puppy, handing him an orange and turning the bruise away from view. The younger kids crowded around the horse, petting his neck and nose and sides. Stains of sweat darkened his deep, chestnut-red hair, and the skin on his legs and flanks twitched with tension.

"How's Action?" Hunter asked. He hooked a finger into the water jug and tipped it up, taking a long swallow. Water dribbled out at the sides of his mouth as he gulped.

"I think he's a little better today, maybe," Mommy said. She couldn't help looking at Cory again, at the frilly white dress. "What's going on?"

"Long story," Hunter said again and wiped his mouth with the back of his hand. "Let me check on Action, and we'll tell you all about it."

Hunter handed the jug to Mommy, and hurried to the trailer. Cory began unhitching the chariot, and took a look at the young kids. "You're Baby, right? Find something to rub the horse with, like a T-shirt," Cory said. "He's all sweaty and we have to dry him off or he'll catch a cold."

"I'll do it!" Teddy Bear said.

"No, me! The princess asked me!" Baby shouted. The two of them ran neck and neck back to the trailer, with Doll racing to catch up.

Angerman folded his arms. "Well, Princess. I thought I burned that place down. I guess I didn't do such a good job if you're here."

Before Mommy could register her surprise at that, Cory led the horse out between the rails of the chariot and so close past Angerman that he had to jump backward to avoid being stepped on.

"My name isn't Princess," Cory said. "And you only burned half of it down."

Kitty was trying to reach up to the horse's neck. Cory lifted the little girl up and set her on the animal's broad back. Kitty settled there with a happy smile while the horse grazed among the weeds, tearing up mouthfuls of green. Then Cory shocked Mommy by kissing Kitty's bare knee. The bruise on her face gave her a wild, dangerous look that jarred with her wedding dress and the tenderness of her kiss.

"Okay," Mommy said in a no-nonsense voice. She was shaken. "We really need to know what's going on here."

"This is my niece," Cory explained. She bent down to Puppy. "And my nephew. I was trying to get them out of the pet shop. I was going to run away with them."

"Wait, wait, a second." Mommy shook her head as if to clear it. "What do you mean they're your niece and nephew? And I thought you were one of them, those Keepers. Why were you going to run away with Puppy and Kitty?"

"They were going to be tested." Cory kicked at the dress tangling her legs. "Anybody got a knife?"

Without a word, Angerman handed her a jackknife. Cory slashed and cut at the hem of her dress until she had hacked off the bottom up to her knees. Then she used the shredded fabric to start rubbing down the horse while it chomped on grass. Green drool gathered in the corners of its mouth as it chewed. When Cory spoke, it was to Teacher and Angerman, and Hunter, too, when he rejoined them. She kept her back turned to Mommy.

"The Keepers are looking for the New Savior, and all they know is it's someone born after the Great Flame. Whenever there are babies, the Keepers wait until they're old enough to walk, and then send them away for Testing. I don't know where, and I don't know what the Testing is—some way of finding out if the kid is the New Savior, I guess. But they don't come back. I guess they all stay there, wherever it is. All I know is, Ingrid didn't want her babies to be tested, so she ran away with them. And somehow you guys brought them back to me, and I had to get them as far away as I could."

"Ingrid?" Teacher asked, her voice sharp.

"My sister." Cory shrugged. "*They* called her Lamentations 1:2. She was one of them, but after the babies she started to act different, like she didn't believe in any of it anymore and wanted people to call her by her old name. And one night she took the babies and ran away."

Mommy shook her head. "Wait a minute, wait a minute. How do you know Puppy and Kitty are Ingrid's children?"

"Because they told me," Cory replied. She wiped

down the horse's forehead, swiping carefully between his eyes. She still didn't look at Mommy.

Angerman laughed. "Yeah, right. They *told* you."

"I asked them what their real mommy's name was, and they said Ingrid."

A dizzy, spinning cloud swirled through Mommy's head. "Wait," she kept whispering. "Wait a minute."

Teacher took Kitty's hand and looked up at her. The little girl sat on the horse's back, smiling first at Cory and then at Mommy. "Kitty?"

Mommy felt a tug at her side. Puppy was pulling on her shirt and looking up at her. She squatted down to his eye level. "What is it, honey?"

"We're still here," Puppy said.

"We're still here," Kitty repeated, as if it were a phrase they had both memorized.

Mommy stared at them. Should she be jealous, because they had spoken to Cory and not to her? Or happy, because they really could talk? She didn't know what to say. She could hear her heart hammering in her ears.

"Hey!" Angerman snapped his fingers. "I saw that, too! The big sign written on the highway outside Lazarus. We're Still Here. I saw that and that's why I stopped there—to see if someone was still alive."

Hunter nodded. "I did that in like the first year after Fire-us—the Great Flame," he added for Cory's benefit. "I guess I thought maybe if there were still people in airplanes they'd see it from up high. I wrote in big letters in white paint on the road."

"Ingrid must've seen it, too," Teacher said.

"So she brought the twins to your town herself?"

Cory asked, her eyes widening. "Did you see her? Why did she . . ."

"She got hot."

They all turned to look at Kitty, who was playing with the horse's mane. Kitty frowned, concentrating on her task. "Ingrid got hot and lie-ded down."

Mommy felt as though the earth were slipping away under her feet. Ingrid got hot. Ingrid got sick, and died, and it must have been somewhere very nearby their old home. Somewhere in Lazarus, maybe even down the street, while Mommy and Teacher and the little ones were living in their house, Ingrid lay down alone and died, and her children wandered away. Her heart seemed to clench inside her rib cage. Mommy looked at Cory, who stood perfectly still.

"Cory—" Mommy reached out to her without thinking.

But Cory flinched and strode away, the ragged hem of her wedding dress bending the grasses as she went.

Chapter Fourteen

"Okay, listen up, here's the plan," Hunter announced.

Angerman glanced up. He, Mommy, Teacher, and the little ones were sprawled out on the grass behind the tractor-trailer, finishing their breakfast of oranges and breath mints and water. Cory was sitting a few steps away, plucking tiny white seed pearls from her wedding dress and flicking them into the weeds. She wouldn't look at anyone. Nearby, a crow preened its feathers and eyed the children, cocking its head.

Hunter was harnessing the red horse again and addressing the group at the same time. Angerman could tell that the boy was anxious to go.

"We've gotta get out of here," Hunter said. "We know the Keepers have three other chariots. Two of them were seen headed south. I was thinking maybe their objective was Lazarus, because—"

He stopped and glanced quickly at Cory. Puppy and Kitty left Mommy's side, crawled over to Cory, and climbed onto her lap. Cory wrapped her arms around them and kissed their heads. A pained expression crossed Mommy's face.

"Anyway, um, and the third chariot went to Pittsburgh," Hunter went on.

Baby rolled her eyes. "Oh, Hunter. It's Pisgah! By the frame!"

"Never say that!" Mommy cried out. "Never use that

expression, do you hear me, Baby?"

Baby pouted. "So-rry."

Hunter tightened one leather strap. "Pisgah. Which means that until one or more of those chariots return to the Crossroads, it'll be hard for the Keepers to follow us. So we can get a good head start on 'em."

Angerman dug his thumbs into his orange and tore the skin apart. He raised the orange to his lips.

Bad Guy peered over Angerman's shoulder. *Ooooh, looks delish! Give me some of that, willya, son?*

"Shuddup," Angerman muttered under his breath.

Teddy Bear stared at Angerman. Angerman smiled at him. "Want some of this orange, Ted?"

"Nothankyou," Teddy Bear whispered, threading his arm through Teacher's.

"I'll ride the horse, and Action can ride in the chariot," Hunter said, straightening up. He glanced briefly at his brother, who was lying on the grass with his eyes half-closed. "Cory, you'll have to ride Action's bike," he added. "The rest of you can stay on the bikes you've got."

Say, I like this guy! Bad Guy exclaimed. *He's got leadership potential!*

Angerman ignored him.

You're just mad because he's the smart one, Bad Guy jeered. *He's always been Mommy's favorite, hasn't he? Mommy's favorite, Mommy's favorite . . .*

Angerman squeezed his orange so hard that the juice began dripping down his bare arms. He tossed it to the ground. Then he reached around, pulled Bad Guy out of his backpack, and shoved its face into the orange.

Mmffgghh!

"You wanted an orange, you got an orange,"

Angerman hissed. He squeezed down on Bad Guy's neck and ground its face back and forth in the pulpy mess.

It felt good. Angerman squeezed even harder. But then he became aware of the total silence around him.

He looked up and saw that everyone was staring at him.

"Don't worry—we used to do this all the time in prep school," Angerman explained.

Teddy Bear's expression brightened. "Prep school? That like Teacher's School?"

"Yeah, except for there's uniforms and dining halls and teas, and . . ." Angerman hesitated. Where was he getting all this from? Did he go to this thing called prep school in the Before Time? Or did someone tell him about it?

"Sun's getting higher," Cory spoke up.

Angerman turned around to look at her. Puppy and Kitty were sitting on either side of her now, playing tug-of-war with the satin sash of her dress. The Princess. Corinthians 1:19. Puppy and Kitty's aunt.

She met his eyes for a second and then lifted her face to the sky. "We should go before it gets too hot."

"Wh-what about your dress?" Mommy pointed out. "And what about your feet? You need shoes."

Cory ignored her. Mommy blushed and turned away. Angerman glanced back and forth between them, at the ugly purple welt on Cory's cheek, and wondered what had gone down between the two girls back at the Crossroads.

Hunter cleared his throat. "Um, there's a bunch of shoes on the truck. Cory, why don't you grab a pair that fits?"

Cory stood up and brushed her hands across her dress, leaving dirt and orange-juice streaks. "Great. Let's go."

The little kids rose to their feet with a lot of moaning and groaning. Angerman knew that no one was looking forward to another long, hot day of scenic bike touring along I-95. He sure wasn't, especially not with the crazy old man on his back who seemed to weigh more and more every day, despite the fact that Angerman had amputated its limbs every chance he got. He wondered if it would be possible to amputate its mouth.

Twenty minutes later, after everyone who needed to had peed and backpacks had been gathered, they hit the road. They rode past buildings, palm trees, faded and peeling billboards: TIRED OF YOUR COMMUTE? QUIT SMOKING TODAY! RODRIGUEZ FOR STATE COMPTROLLER. Everything looked so normal, and yet not so normal. Cars were crashed at the side of the road. Kudzu and other weeds grew over everything, like a horrible green carpet. Everything had had five years to rot, fade, decay, crumble, crack, slip, and rust. For five years wind, rain, sun, and storm, leaf and tendril, dust and death had worked hard to erase all sign of human civilization from the landscape.

Hunter led the caravan on the red horse, going along at a trot so that Action Figure, asleep, wouldn't tumble out of the open back of the chariot. Behind the chariot were Mommy with Kitty in the kid seat, and Teacher with Puppy, followed by the rest of the little ones.

Angerman and Cory were in the way back. Cory had gathered up the hem of her wedding dress in a big, awkward knot to keep it out of the way, and she was wearing a pair of shiny white sneakers from the truck.

Angerman sidled up next to her. "Hey, Princess," he said.

Cory glared at him. "What do you want, Angry Man?"

"That's Angerman. Get it right. Nothing I hate more than having someone get my name wrong."

Cory guffawed. "That your real name? *Angerman?* What, your mother was having a bad day when she gave birth to you?"

Bad Guy began laughing hysterically.

"Shuddup!" Angerman cried out to both of them.

"I'm sorry, I didn't mean . . ." Cory looked apologetic.

Angerman gripped the handlebars very tight. He could smell the rotting orange-juice smell wafting from Bad Guy, and tried to squelch a wave of nausea.

"Don't worry about it."

From somewhere deep in the recesses of Angerman's memory, some words came to him: *His eyes were as a flame of fire, and on his head were many crowns; and he had a name written, that no man knew, but he himself.* He saw sunlight slanting through jeweled windows, making red and purple and green flecks dance across the hard wooden chairs. He saw a man in a white robe. He saw a large gold cross. He saw people in dark suits with curly wires going into their ears, and they were whispering behind their hands. He saw . . . no, he *felt* . . . a warm hand covering his own and squeezing it lightly. And he heard a voice whispering, "Sit still, it's almost over now."

Brothers and sisters, amen! Bad Guy cried out.

"Quiet," Angerman hissed.

Cory frowned at him. Angerman smiled. "Sooooo. You're Puppy and Kitty's aunt, huh?"

Cory gazed ahead at Puppy and Kitty sitting in their kid's bike seats. "They take after . . . they have the same color eyes as my mom."

"Your parents died of Fire-us? The Great Flame, I mean."

"Car accident. The year before."

Angerman considered this. There was so much he wanted to know about Puppy and Kitty, about Ingrid, about the Keepers, about this thing called the "New Savior." He didn't know why, but ever since he'd seen the words We're Still Here painted across the highway going through Lazarus, ever since he'd found Mommy and the others, he'd been filled with a sense of . . . what? Destiny, fate, something-meant-to-be. He was meant to be with this family, he was meant to lead them to Washington to find President. And it was all tied up with the twins, with the Keepers. But he wasn't sure how.

"How much do you know about those wackos you were living with?" Angerman asked Cory.

Cory tossed her long blond braid over her shoulder. "You mean the Keepers?"

My favorite subject! Bad Guy interrupted. *Keepers for $200. Bob, we have some beautiful prizes for our contestants today, including a hibachi grill, a brand-new Chef-Magik stove, AND a pressure cooker guaranteed to cook the bejeezus out of—*

"Stop it, stop it!" Angerman cried out.

Cory frowned. "What? I didn't do anything!"

"And thou shalt say unto them, This is the offering made by fire which ye shall offer unto the Lord; two

lambs of the first year without spot day by day, for a continual burnt offering." Mmm, love those lamb chops! By the flame!

"STOP IT!"

White-hot rage washed over Angerman, making his head spin, blinding him. He stood up on his bike and pedaled harder, faster, wishing Bad Guy would just go flying off his back and into the air and land in a ditch somewhere, to die. He pedaled so hard and so fast that he passed the little ones, who all stared at him like he was a freak, and Mommy and Teacher, ditto, and even the chariot and the red horse. "Angerman?" Mommy called after him. "You all right?" But he didn't answer her.

Wheeeeeeee! Bad Guy shouted. *Hey, what's that up ahead? Looks like a party! Are we invited?*

Angerman skidded to a halt and put his right foot out to prop himself up. Just ahead of them on the highway was a wall of smashed-up cars and jack-knifed trucks. The highway curved around, so Angerman could see that the pile-up continued for at least a mile or so. A rattlesnake slithered out of sight beneath a car with a warning *bzzz* of its tail.

Angerman sucked in a deep breath and inched his bike a little closer to the wreckage. Nearby, next to an overturned red minivan, was a skeleton in faded jeans and a Budweiser T-shirt. There were more skeletons up ahead, lying on the pavement or falling out of cars, their clothes rotting away. It looked like a battlefield.

The others had all stopped behind him and were regarding the carnage in stunned silence. Angerman smiled. "This just in! We have a live news bulletin from our TrafficCam crew. There's major congestion on I-95 north of Jacksonville, by the Flame!"

"Angerman!" Hunter warned.

Still smiling, Angerman turned and began walking his bike through the wrecked cars and the skeletons. His tires crunched over a leg bone, and it snapped in two. "Yay! Though I walk through the valley of the shadow of death, I will fear no evil: for I am WITH ME!" he shouted, pumping his fist in the air.

Behind him, the younger children began wailing with fear.

They proceeded through the graveyard of cars and bones. Cory led the way on her bike, followed by the chariot, followed by everyone else. Angerman had stopped in the middle of his insane speech, leaned against an upside-down station wagon that said JUST MARRIED on it, and burst into tears. Now he was walking his bike, way in back.

It was horrible, horrible. Cory felt like leaning against something and bursting into tears, herself. There were skeletons everywhere—grown-up skeletons, kid skeletons, baby skeletons—not to mention skulls, leg bones, arm bones, bones scattered by animals. Hats, pocketbooks, unidentifiable sodden belongings lay among the dead. It made her think of the ride to the Crossroads with Ingrid, five years ago. *Close your eyes, it's better not to see.* Except Cory couldn't close her eyes now. None of them could. They had to keep going and try to get to the other side.

If they could get to the other side. It was hard to find a clear path through the wreckage. The chariot especially had a hard time passing through. It was too wide, and its sides kept scraping and grinding against the sides of cars. The poor horse was wide-eyed with alarm, whinnying and tossing its mane and kicking up its hooves. From the hood of a sports car, a rattlesnake flicked its tongue at them.

The little ones were hysterical, sobbing and screaming with each new skeleton they had to pass. Hunter had told her that the little ones had never seen the dead, because he had always managed to hide them first. "Sweeping for bones," he'd called it.

Bones. That's all Ingrid would be soon. Cory's eyes filled with tears, and for a moment, the sea of death around her became washed-out and blurry.

Something yanked at Cory's dress. She swiped at her eyes and glanced down. The ragged hem of her wedding dress had become caught in the spokes of her wheel. She reached down and pulled it, hard. There was a ripping noise, and black grease smeared across the white fabric.

At that moment, an image from her Visioning came to her: Stumbling down the dark road, her wedding dress getting caught on rocks and brambles. What had the owl said to her?

Near the wheel of her bike was a baby's car seat, bleached white from the sun. A small, intact skeleton was strapped onto it, a rubber pacifier on a cord around its neck. Cory kicked it out of the way, before the others could see.

"Hunter, how much farther?" Mommy called out. Her voice was husky from crying.

"Can't tell," Hunter replied. "If it goes on like this,

we'll have to leave the chariot behind. I could carry Action . . ."

He turned around and frowned at his brother, who was sprawled on the platform of the chariot. Even Cory could tell that the young boy didn't look well. His face was ghostly white, and his hair was matted with sweat. He didn't look too far from being bones himself.

"Mommy!" Doll wailed. "Mommy, I wanna go home!"

"Hang on, we're almost there!" Mommy said, her voice breaking. "Let's sing a song—who wants to sing a song?"

"It's impossible to see if there's a clear path ahead," Hunter said to no one in particular.

A clear path. They needed a clear path.

Cory closed her eyes, trying to remember. What had the owl said?

And then it came to her. *Take off the veil.*

Cory opened her eyes. Her veil *was* off. She had taken it off when she and Hunter escaped from the Crossroads. She should be able to see now: see her clear path; see a clear path for them all.

"Wait!"

She was surprised by the strong, sure sound of her own voice, ringing out above the children's sobs and the scraping and grinding of the chariot against the sides of cars. "Wait, I have an idea. Everyone stop for a second, okay?"

Cory got off her bike, popped the kickstand, and ran over to an overturned tractor-trailer. She started climbing to the top of it.

"Cory, what are you doing?" Hunter called out.

"Getting us out of here," she replied.

Cory reached the top of the cabin and gazed out at the valley of death. From the high vantage point, she could make out a path—a clear path—through which the chariot would be able to pass. Around the blue station wagon, straight ahead to the white convertible, then . . . She committed it to memory, nodded to herself, and climbed back down.

Everyone was staring at her as she walked up to Hunter. "I found a way out," she announced breathlessly. "Hunter, if you'll take my bike, I can take the horse and lead us out of here. Okay?"

Hunter looked at her in surprise, and then scrambled down. "Okay."

Cory took the horse's reins in her hands and started to guide it around the overturned tractor-trailer. She glanced up at the sky and smiled. "I'll make sure your children are safe," she whispered. "I promise." And she began leading her niece and nephew and the rest of the family out of the valley of death, out of the shadows, and into the light.

Chapter Fifteen

They spent a restless night at the Seaspray Inn. By the time they had stumbled into the blue-carpeted lobby at the end of the day, the children were exhausted and nearly sick from crying. Mommy, Teacher, Cory, and Angerman had found beds and blankets for everyone as fast as possible, while Hunter carried Action Figure in from the chariot and laid him on a couch in the reception area. With a frightened glance back at his sick brother, Hunter had gone out to unharness the horse and rub it down the way he'd seen the Keepers do at the Daily Strengthening. A fenced area just outside the "This Way to the Garden" door served as a corral for the horse, and he had left it there, munching on grass and flowers, just before he stumbled inside and fell asleep on the blue carpeting beside Action Figure.

His muscles twitching with fatigue, his head jangling, Hunter fell in and out of unconsciousness. He was so deeply tired that he felt as if he were falling backward into darkness every time he closed his eyes. Always, within minutes, he jerked awake and reached his hand up to the sofa to touch Action Figure, to check if he was still breathing. After wading through that river of bones, Hunter had an unshakable fear that Action Figure was going to die during the night. Each time he awoke he lay rigid in the dark, waiting for the speed of his heartbeat to settle down. He could hear the cries and whimpers of bad dreams from the other rooms in the tiny inn. When the windows of the lobby began to lighten, Hunter finally lost the struggle, and slept hard. No dreams. No death.

He plunged upward into the light when he heard Action Figure's voice.

"Hunna?" the boy whispered.

"Yeah? I'm awake," Hunter said, struggling to sit up.

Sunlight was streaming in through the windows on the east side of the lobby, touching Action Figure's skinny body. The boy was lying on his side, his eyes half open. He licked his lips.

"Do you want something?" Hunter asked. He fumbled for his glasses and shoved them onto his face. "Water? How about some water?"

He heard a footstep behind him and he glanced around. Mommy was tiptoeing out of a bedroom, shutting the door carefully behind her. She gave Hunter and Action Figure a warm smile, a Mommy smile.

"Hey, how are you feeling?" she whispered. She kneeled beside the sofa and put one hand to Action Figure's forehead. He was too weak to try to jerk his head away. His lips moved, and he muttered something and closed his eyes. Mommy and Hunter exchanged a worried glance. Hunter felt his stomach lurch. Action Figure was dying. He was dying.

"What'd you say?" Hunter asked.

With a great effort, Action Figure said, "Man."

"Man?" Mommy repeated. "Angerman? Is that what you mean? What man?"

Understanding rushed through Hunter. Tears stung his eyes, and he blinked them back. "You want to be a man, is that it?"

Action Figure's eyes glowed for a moment. Slowly, once, he nodded his head. Mommy looked at Hunter, at a loss. He stood up and beckoned to her. His heart thudding, he led her a few steps away to stand by the registration desk. A clear plastic brochure stand on the counter held three sagging cards that read, *Tell us about your visit! Your comments help us serve you better!*

"What is it—what does he want?" Mommy asked, a crease of worry between her eyebrows.

Remorse had Hunter by the heart. "I gave him a hard time, back there at the Crossroads. Made him think he wasn't—isn't a man, just a kid," Hunter said. He couldn't bring himself to look at Mommy. "I think he's afraid he'll never get to grow up—now he's sick and it's all my fault."

"Oh, no, no," Mommy said. She put one hand on his arm. "Hunter, it's not your fault he's sick."

Hunter's head was spinning. In spite of it all, the grief, the self-hate, he was looking at Mommy's hand on his arm, and hating himself even more because it made him happy. He wanted her to say his name again in that same tender way and keep her hand there. He was disgusted with himself.

A noise from the couch caught his ear. Hunter and Mommy both turned, and for a moment of glad surprise they didn't speak. Action Figure had dragged his knapsack up onto the couch with him, and he was eating something from inside it.

"Hey, you're eating!" Hunter took three long strides toward the sofa. "We've got oranges, too, if you're hungry—"

Action Figure hunched over his knapsack, trying weakly to stuff whatever was inside down out of sight. His throat bulged as he swallowed, and he gagged a little bit but swallowed again.

Hunter felt cold. "What are you eating?" he demanded.

With one swift movement, he grabbed the knapsack from his brother's grasp. He tucked it under one arm as he dug into it with his other hand. His fingers closed around a jar as Action Figure fell back exhausted on the couch. "What is this?"

Mommy was at his side as he turned it around to read the label. "*Man Power*?" Hunter read. "*Nutritional supplement*? What the—?"

Mommy reached out one finger and pointed at the picture on the label, a glistening, muscle-packed man flexing his massive biceps. She looked up and met Hunter's astonished gaze. "To make him a man."

"You've been eating this?" Hunter gasped. "Action, that won't—I mean, you can't—" At a loss for words, he twisted off the lid of the jar. It was some kind of powder, and the jar was half empty. Within moments of opening the jar, Hunter noticed a musty smell. Cautiously, he tipped his face to sniff the jar and then jerked away. He held it toward the light of the windows and turned it to let the powder sift back and forth—there were threads of mold growing throughout it. He and Mommy looked at it for a moment, and then Hunter threw it across the room. The powder sprayed along the wall, leaving a greenish stain.

"Action, this is making you sick!" Hunter cried out. "How long have you been eating this?"

But he knew. They'd all noticed Action Figure becoming lethargic and silent back at the Crossroads. But they had ignored it, each of them secretly relieved to have the wild Action Figure quiet down while they planned their escape. Hunter felt a great howl welling up inside his chest. He picked up a wooden chair and flung it as hard as he could into the wall. It smashed into a floor lamp and knocked a framed picture of daisies off its hook.

"Come on," Mommy said. "Help me get him outside."

Hunter couldn't move. Guilt and despair had turned him to stone. All he could do was stand empty-handed and useless and watch Mommy trying to lift Action Figure off the couch.

"Help me!" Mommy said, her voice sharp as the boy tried to squirm away from her.

Hunter stumbled forward and shoved one arm under his brother's knees and another behind his shoulders. Action Figure felt as light as a pile of bones. Mommy pushed open the "This Way to the Garden" door, and Hunter followed her outside into the sunshine. The bright light hurt Action Figure's eyes, and he pressed his face against Hunter's chest. Tiny birds chirped among the overgrown flowers, and a giant blue butterfly fanned its wings on an overturned sundial.

"We have to make him throw up," Mommy said. "Put him down."

While they arranged Action Figure's limp body on

the ground, the red horse stood watching them from the other end of the garden. Hunter did what he was told, holding his brother's shoulders while Mommy opened Action Figure's mouth and stuck her finger down his throat. The boy struggled and gagged, but Mommy did it again.

Hunter felt Action Figure's body heave as he lunged forward, vomiting onto the grass. Action Figure began to cry, and vomited again. Mommy looked at Hunter over Action Figure's head. "Get some water. Okay, it's okay," she said, turning back to Action Figure. "You're gonna get better now."

Almost without knowing what he did, Hunter blundered back into the lobby, his vision blurred with tears. There were water bottles somewhere, over there on that table where he'd left them. Hunter swept the empty ones to the floor, searching for the heaviness of a full bottle. As he gripped the neck of a bottle that had water in it, he felt himself go weak at the knees and he sat down hard on the floor.

He could hear the murmur of voices down the hall, Teacher's voice and Angerman's, no doubt talking to the younger kids and telling them everything was all right. All right.

But it was never *all right*. They lived in constant fear. Sometimes Hunter didn't know how any of them had survived so long. How easy it would be, how sudden, for one of them not to be alive.

Hunter pushed himself up and went back to the garden door. Through the opening he saw Mommy sitting on the overgrown grass, cradling Action Figure in her arms. And while Hunter watched, the red horse ambled toward them, breathing loud puffs of air through its nostrils as it took in the scent of the two children. Head low, it stopped beside Mommy and Action Figure.

The sick boy raised one hand to the horse's muzzle, and the animal made a soft *hmm-hmm-hmm* sound deep in its throat. Mommy turned her face toward the lobby door, saw Hunter, and gave him the most beautiful smile he had ever seen.

A thick bank of clouds had rolled in from the east on a salty breeze. It was cooler with the sun hidden, and the sorrows of the last day felt easier to bear. Teacher pumped her legs up and down, up and down in a steady rhythm, trying to match the beat of the horse's trotting hooves as they continued north up the interstate. From the corner of her eye, she saw a white blur moving up into position beside her.

Teacher gave Cory a nod in greeting. She couldn't help noticing that Cory's wedding dress was a problem for her, even though Cory had ripped out the sleeves and hacked off much of the full skirt. The fancy embroidery and ribbons were dirty and raveled, and Cory had tied the satin sash around her forehead as a sweatband. Loose threads hung like a fringe from the armholes, tossing and blowing in the breeze. Cory looked like— Teacher searched her memory, and the word *pirate* came to mind. She thought there might be a picture of a *pirate* somewhere in The Book, but when her thoughts flipped through the pages, she felt a pulling away, a retreat, as though The Book didn't want to be read. She frowned.

"I want to ask you something," Cory said, and when Teacher nodded, she went on. "Back at the Crossroads.

They were going to burn your book thing, right?"

Teacher's scowl deepened.

"I didn't give it to them, I swear by the Fl— I swear," Cory corrected herself. "You gotta believe me, I wouldn't ever have done that. Somebody else stole it, not me. Probably you-know-who. Ruth 2:10, that sneak."

"You wanted to steal it, though," Teacher said.

Cory sat up, riding no-handed while she straightened her back. "I just wanted to look at it. I had to see if it had my answers."

"Why would you find your answers in our Book? It's *our* Book, for *our* answers," Teacher said, her voice rising.

The other girl gave her a doubtful look. "Yeah, but I don't have any books at all. Yours is the only one I have ever seen. I thought—since my Vision had this book in it and we didn't have any books at the Crossroads, and then you showed up with a book, so I figured . . ."

Teacher swerved a bit as she turned her head to stare at Cory riding alongside. "Your what?"

"My Vision. Don't you know about your Visioning? Nobody ever told you about it?"

"I never heard of it," Teacher said. She made a face and watched a pelican row through the air. "We had to learn everything ourselves. There's lots we don't know. I have to find Information and put it in The Book, and that's how we know things, like about lunch specials, and Ten Commandments, and about aspirin and stuff. But I never found anything about Visioning."

Cory looked surprised. "I didn't know you had to write the books yourself. I thought they came that way. With words inside."

"Most of them do. Anyway, they used to in the Before Time," Teacher said. "You really never saw a book before?"

"Nope. I mean, I know I did in the—what you call Before Time. We always called it Before the Great Flame. But I don't really remember it somehow. I kinda remember, but it's real misty. So when I saw the book in my Vision I knew what it was, and I knew I was supposed to read it."

Teacher was more and more intrigued. "What did it say?"

Cory looked away. "I'm not a real good reader," she admitted. "I can read some words and stuff, but since we didn't have books all I could practice on was signs and things that were still at the Crossroads. I guess that's how come I couldn't read the book in my Vision—like I could see the words, but they didn't make any sense. Or like I didn't have enough time to spell out the sounds. I know it's real important, whatever it says in there, though. It's supposed to tell me about my path."

The certainty in Cory's voice made Teacher feel small and weak. She had never felt so confident about the messages in The Book. Almost without fail, every time she read The Book the meanings were cloudy to her, and she had to feel her way like someone walking through the dark.

So . . . what if The Book really was Cory's book? Teacher was worried about this Visioning thing. It sounded very important, and she felt alarmed and embarrassed that she hadn't known about it already. There was so much she didn't know! It was so hard to find Information and understand it! Maybe from the very beginning of everything, Teacher had been making The Book just to bring it to Cory. And that strange message she had found in it, maybe it was telling her that it wasn't hers to look at anymore, that it was time to hand it over.

But if that were true, then Teacher would have no meaning anymore. For as long as she could remember, since Fire-us, her most important task was to keep The Book, to use it to teach the family about the Before Time, to help them remember how to be human beings. If she had to give up The Book, she wouldn't be Teacher anymore. She would be . . . nothing.

"So, I was hoping," Cory went on when Teacher stayed silent. "I was hoping you'd let me look at it. To see if it tells me my path."

Teacher began shaking her head. "No," she whispered. "No, you can't." Then she stood on her pedals, speeding up to leave Cory behind.

Chapter Sixteen

Angerman was in a sort of trance as they got off the interstate.
Bad Guy had been jabbering at him all day, and all last
night, too—ever since the pileup just north of
Jacksonville. The jabbering was really bad, worse than
usual, and the only strategy Angerman had figured
out—so he wouldn't lose his mind completely and maybe
start throwing bikes off an overpass or something—was
to keep doing the News over and over again.

"This just in! A baby panda was born today at the
National Zoo. Its parents, Mei Ling and Fourier, were
gifts from the People's Republic of China in 1995. Zoo
officials announced that mother and baby are both doing
well, and—"

*What about the Testing? Gotta test those babies, by
the Flame!*

"—will be available for public viewing in a couple of
days."

*What DOES one wear to a Testing? Gosh, I think my
tuxedo's being cleaned!*

"And on the other side of the globe, in Sydney,
Australia . . ."

Mommy, who had been riding alongside Hunter and
the red horse, slowed down until she was side by side
with Angerman. She smiled at him, then she looked into
his eyes. Her smile disappeared. "Angerman? You
okay?"

"Fine, I'm just fine!" he boomed. "Thanks for asking! Nice weather we're having, isn't it? Tonight, expect a low of sixty-three degrees, with a thirty percent chance of rain."

"Yeah, well . . ." Mommy brushed back her hair and glanced at Hunter. "We were talking, and Hunter was saying we should look for a place to spend the night. It's getting late. The kids are tired."

If Hunter says so, that's good enough for me! Hunter, Hunter, he's our man! Hunter in 2008!

"If Hunter says so, that's . . . that is . . . at the Dew Drop Inn, kids under twelve sleep for free. Complimentary continental breakfast included. Enjoy our heated pool and Jacuzzi . . ."

Angerman continued to babble, even though he could see that Mommy's eyes were getting bigger and bigger, even though he knew he was acting like a lunatic. He *knew*—that was the worst part. It was as if half his brain was out there, out of control, a runaway train, while the other half of his brain was forced to witness everything and yet was helpless to do anything.

Hard to charm the ladies when you don't have all your marbles, ain't it, son? Politics is all about charm, winning friends, and influencing people.

Angerman's arm shot out to grab Bad Guy, but he stopped himself just in time. His arm dangled in the air as he coasted down a small hill, as if he were signaling to make a turn. A turn to nowhere. He clenched and unclenched his fist, and felt the warm wind blowing through his fingers.

Mommy coasted beside him and stared at his fist. "What're you doing?"

There was a billboard, off to the right. It had a picture of a soldier on horseback and gray letters against a faded white background:

THE BATTLE OF THE SALT PANS
CIVIL WAR LIVING HISTORY
MUSEUM
FUN FOR THE WHOLE FAMILY!
AHEAD 1.2 MILES

Angerman pointed to the billboard with his dangling arm, as if he'd intended to do that all along. "Check that out," he said to Mommy, jabbing a finger.

"'The Battle of the Salt Pans,'" Mommy read.

A thought occurred to Angerman. "Hey! We should stay there. Spend the night, I mean."

Mommy nodded. "That's a good idea. The kids would like it."

Angerman's heart swelled unexpectedly at the praise in Mommy's words. She liked his suggestion! He was useful to the family! "Okay, cool. I'll go up ahead and tell Hunter, and I can lead the way there."

"Great. I'll tell the others."

Mommy fell back to where Teacher and Teddy Bear and the girls were riding. Cory was way in back. Angerman sped up until he had caught up to the horse and chariot.

Hunter glanced over, the reins in one hand. The horse was shiny with sweat, and its breath was coming out in quick, rhythmic snorts. "Hey, what's up?"

"Mommy and I've been talking," Angerman announced. "And Mommy and I decided that the family should spend the night at the Civil War museum place."

Hunter bristled. "What Civil War museum place?"

"Horse," Action Figure called out. The boy was kneeling in the chariot, looking out at the landscape. "Man on a horse."

"That's right, Action! You didn't see the sign, Hunter? Gosh! Too busy being on your high red horse? Well, anyway, Mommy and I saw it, and Mommy and I decided that it would be a good place for the kids. Don't worry, Mommy and I know the way."

Without waiting for a reply from Hunter, Angerman stood up on his bike and pedaled ahead. A salty breeze blew through his hair, which he'd tied back with a blue bandanna from Banana Republic. He began whistling.

The road was clear—no smashed-up cars or bones. Behind him, he could hear the steady clip-clop of Hunter's horse, the wheels of the chariot, the high rise of the kids' voices: "Mommy, are we there yet? Mommy, whatsa mew-see-um? Mommy, will there be food for us to eat?"

"This just in! Four score and seven years ago our fathers brought forth on this continent, a new nation . . ." Angerman said out loud.

And five years ago our Father brought forth on this continent a new nation, too! Whoopee!

". . . a new nation, conceived in liturgy and dedicated to the contradiction that all men are created equal. And in Superbowl news: This Sunday, the Redskins will take on the Giants in what should be the battle of the century . . ."

Angerman saw the sign just ahead: BATTLE OF THE SALT PANS LIVING HISTORY MUSEUM. He squeezed his brakes to slow down. Off to the right was an enormous parking lot overgrown with weeds, a few cars, and a cluster of small wooden buildings nestled among palm and peach trees. The buildings didn't look anything like the ones they'd seen in Jacksonville. Dozens of seagulls were lined up on the ridges of the houses, facing every which way and quarreling with each other.

Angerman thrust his legs out so that he wasn't pedaling anymore. *Wheee, look Sam, no feet!* He had said that to someone a long time ago. He steered the bike into the parking lot and waved for the rest of the family to do the same.

"This way! Come on!"

He stopped and jumped off his bike and leaned it against a peach tree. The branches were weighed down with rotting fruit, and tiny flies buzzed everywhere. Mommy, Teacher, Cory, and the little ones all parked their bikes nearby. Hunter stopped the horse on the other side of the lot and tied the horse to a utility pole. He held out his arms and lifted Action Figure out of the chariot.

"Mew-see-um!"

The kids spilled through a gate and scattered toward the wooden buildings, laughing and shouting. Angerman's eyes lingered on Puppy and Kitty, who were trying to catch up to Baby and Doll and Teddy Bear. He noticed that Cory was also watching them. She was still dressed in her white princess dress, although she had torn the sleeves off and most of the skirt, too.

Mommy, Teacher, Hunter, Cory, and Angerman followed after the little ones. Hunter carried Action Figure in his arms.

"Puh me down!" Action Figure demanded.

"You're not strong enough yet," Hunter insisted.

"Puh me down!" Action Figure began wriggling and thrashing like a wild animal. Strong enough to sock Hunter in the chin, anyway.

Hunter grunted and lowered his brother to the ground. Action Figure started to run after the other little kids, then stumbled. Hunter reached out to grab him.

"Lemme go!" Hunter let go, and Action Figure began half walking, half limping toward a building with a sign over it that said: NATHANIEL GIBBON, GUNSMITH.

Mommy touched Hunter and whispered something in his ear. Hunter smiled and nodded.

"What *is* this place?" Cory said, looking around.

"Can't you read the sign, Princess?" Angerman snapped. "It's the Battle of the Salt Pans Civil War Living History Museum."

"What does The Book say about this Civil War thing?" Mommy asked Teacher.

Teacher hugged The Book to her chest but didn't look at it. "I already know about the Civil War. It took place about two or three or four hundred years ago, in Vietnam. People tried to escape the war, and a man named Abraham parted the Red Sea so they could get away. But the people died, anyway."

Mommy exhaled sharply. "Oh."

That these dead shall not have died in vain—that this nation, under God, shall have a new birth of fiefdom—and that government of the peephole, by the peephole, for the peephole, shall not perish from the earth!

It was chattering in his ear again. Angerman clenched his teeth and smiled at the others and said, "This just in! Confederate President Jefferson Davis was captured in Georgia. Union soldiers put him in shackles and dragged him to prison, where rats are regularly consumed for breakfast, lunch, and dinner. *Bon appetite*, Jeff! And, hey, presidents are having a tough time everywhere! At Ford's Theater in Washington, District of Columbia, President Abraham Lincoln was shot and killed by John Wilkes Booth, who shouted '*Sic semper tyrannis!*' after he plugged a bullet into the old man's head. *Sic semper tyrannis*—that means 'So be it always to tyrants,' in case your Latin's a little rusty. A bullet into the old man's head . . . *pop!* . . . Just like that!" He raised a finger over his head, pointed it at his backpack, and pretended to shoot.

Before anyone could respond, Baby and Doll spilled out of one of the wooden buildings, giggling. They were dressed in gray soldier's coats that dragged behind their heels. Teddy Bear was right behind them, wearing a bright red cap with a brass cross on it. He was waving a sword in the air and shouting "Whoo-hoo!"

"Teddy, put that down before you hurt someone!" Mommy cried out.

"It's not a for-real sword, Mommy. See!" Teddy Bear pushed the sword into the ground. The silver blade buckled and curved.

"We're here with a live report!" Angerman said to no one in particular, then walked into the wooden building.

Inside, there were dozens of glass cases full of weapons—swords, sabers, muskets, revolvers—and uniforms mounted on the walls. Puppy and Kitty were in the corner rooting through a large trunk, pulling out red sashes and leather boots and more play swords. A sign above it said:

PLEASE INVITE YOUR CHILDREN TO ENJOY THESE COSTUMES AND PLAY WEAPONS DURING YOUR VISIT! HOWEVER, PLEASE DON'T ALLOW THEM TO TOUCH THE REAL COSTUMES AND WEAPONS!

While Puppy and Kitty fought over a gray coat with gold buttons, Angerman strode over to one of the glass cases. He took off one of his sneakers and brought it down on the case—*smash!* Puppy and Kitty stopped fighting and stared at him in alarm.

"Just killing a bug," Angerman reassured them, slipping his shoe back on.

Puppy and Kitty said nothing and resumed their tug-of-war games. Angerman reached into the glass case and pulled out a long, thin steel saber. The grip was cool and curved and smooth, and it felt good in his hand. This was no rubber toy.

"Reward: runaway kid," he said in a low voice. "Prime condition except for a streak of bad attitude, fourteen years or thereabouts, answers to the name of Angerman, property of . . . no one." He made a slicing motion in the air. The blade whistled. "Take that, fire-eaters!"

Oooh, I'm scared!

"This just in!" Angerman held the hilt of the saber to his mouth, like a microphone. "You *should* be."

The light was fading, and the first star was twinkling in the pale pink sky. A peach orchard, overgrown with weeds and fragrant with rotted fruit, stretched behind the museum compound. Rabbits moved languidly, ambling forward to nibble the grass and the fallen fruit, and ambling forward again. Overhead, bats flitted between branches, diving for mosquitoes.

Mommy walked among the trees, noticing how pretty it all looked, and recited *"Keep America Beautiful"* to herself. She stooped to gather firewood, trying to keep her eye on Puppy and Kitty at the same time. The twins were carrying play swords and chasing each other around the peach trees. Puppy was dressed in a gray soldier's coat with gold trim, and he had a red sash tied around his head. Kitty had what looked to be a red flag with a blue *X* crisscrossed on it draped over her new Gap Kids dress, like a cape.

"Puppy, careful with that sword! Kitty, pull that red thing up a bit, you're going to trip on it!" Mommy adjusted the load in her arms and wondered, a little irritably, where the others were. She knew Hunter had gone out to look for food and water. But where were Angerman and Teacher?

Maybe they were just looking after the other little ones, she thought. And Teacher—she needed to cut Teacher some slack. Something was troubling her friend deeply, Mommy could see. In fact, as soon as they'd arrived at the Living History Museum, she and Teacher had come upon a building full of brochures and maps. But instead of being happy-crazy, instead of throwing herself into a frenzy of reading and pasting, Teacher had ignored the written things and walked out the door. No explanation, nothing. Something was definitely wrong.

As for Angerman . . . of course the Crossroads had

made him worse. But getting away from the Crossroads didn't seem to have made him better. Mommy leaned over and picked up a stick that would be good for kindling, and sighed. She wished she could understand Angerman, understand what made him so black inside. He needed to be protected, like a child, even though he was almost as big and tall as a man.

The sound of barking and meowing came to her from a distance. She glanced up. "Puppy? Kitty?" she called out.

The twins had gotten a little ways away from her, and were running around and around a palm tree. It was hard to see them in the deepening shadows of the woods. "Puppy, Kitty, get back here!"

"You want some help?"

Mommy turned around. Cory was walking toward her down a narrow dirt path. Mommy gasped at the change in the other girl. Cory had shed her white wedding gown and was dressed head to toe in a cavalry officer's uniform: a long gray coat with gold buttons, matching pants, and brown leather boots that hugged her shins. She had bunched up her long blond braid under a broad-brimmed gray hat. The hat did nothing to hide her cheek, which was still puffy and bruised looking.

Cory noticed Mommy noticing her cheek. "It's getting better, I think."

Mommy opened her mouth, and then clamped it shut again. She didn't know what to say. At last, she managed a rueful, "Cory, I'm sorry—"

Cory jutted her chin at the pile of firewood in Mommy's arms. "You want some help with that? Looks like you've got your hands full. Here, why don't you give me the wood, and you can go after Ingr— after Puppy and Kitty."

"Okay, thanks."

Mommy handed the wood to the other girl, then jogged over to where the twins were playing their tag games. "Puppy, Kitty! Come on; let's go back to the courtyard. It's time to make a fire for dinner—won't that be fun?"

Puppy and Kitty stopped chasing each other and obeyed Mommy. They ran ahead of her toward the courtyard, from where Mommy could now hear the sounds of Baby and Doll singing one of their nonsense songs: "No more pecks of corn, no more diver's eyelashes!" Mommy followed the twins through a small clearing, then past the post office and bank buildings. After a minute, Cory fell in step beside her.

Mommy couldn't help staring at Cory's soldier costume again. She looked so different—*so* different. "Why were you wearing that thing, anyway?" she said. "The wedding dress, I mean."

Cory shifted the wood in her arms and stared straight ahead. "I was being groomed to be a Handmaid."

"What's a Handmaid?"

Cory squashed a rotten peach with the heel of her boot, and ground it into a mushy pulp. "I don't—I don't really know," she muttered. "But all the girls at the Crossroads my age have wedding dresses made for them. Then they're sent away."

Mommy felt cold all of a sudden. "Sent away where?" she whispered.

"I don't know. They never come back. A different

place to live, I guess."

The two girls reached the courtyard. The little ones were all playing together now: Puppy and Kitty, the girls, Teddy Bear, and even Action Figure, who was squatting on the ground and pitching pebbles at a sculpture of a soldier. Teacher was sitting on a wooden bench, watching them quietly. The Book was on her lap, closed.

Angerman was standing over a shallow pit in the ground. He had a black shovel in one hand and a silver saber in the other. "I dug this for you, for the campfire," he called out to Mommy.

Mommy smiled at him. "Thank you! That's great!" She stared at the saber, and wondered if it was one of the fake ones like the little ones were playing with. It looked so real.

Mommy and Cory got busy building the fire. They arranged the sticks and branches in the hole Angerman had dug. Then Mommy got a book of matches out of her pocket and lit the dried leaves and twigs.

The kindling began to crackle. A golden-white flame curled up into the air. Mommy watched it for a second, and then turned to Cory. "You said Ingrid ran away from the Crossroads when Puppy and Kitty were babies," she whispered. "Why do you suppose she did that?"

"I think she was trying to protect them," Cory replied. "All the babies at the Crossroads are taken away when they can walk and talk. They get sent away for the Testing."

"What's the Testing?"

"I don't know. But the babies never come back, and neither do their mommies. Just like the Handmaids."

Mommy stood up and began pacing around the fire,

which was growing bigger. It crackled and snapped as the wood burned hotter. From a distance, she could see Hunter walking toward them from the parking lot, carrying packages and bottles.

Testing. Obviously Puppy and Kitty were taken from her and the rest of the family at the Crossroads so they could be tested. But what did that mean? And would the Keepers continue to try to track Puppy and Kitty down, so they could be tested?

Cory tapped her on the shoulder. "Look, I know you're worried about them. I'm worried about them, too. That's why I had to get them out of the mall . . ."

Mommy had her eyes on Puppy as she listened to Cory. He was too close to the fire, and even as she opened her mouth to warn him, he tripped and stumbled into the flame.

"Puppy!"

Mommy and Cory both ran toward him, but Angerman was closest. He thrust his arms into the fire and scooped the boy up in one swift motion. Then he threw himself and Puppy on the ground and rolled around and around.

By the time Mommy and Cory reached them, the two boys were covered with dirt. Angerman propped Puppy up to a sitting position and scanned him from head to toe. "You okay?" he demanded. "You all right?"

Puppy nodded, tears streaming down his dirty face. "We're still here?"

"We're still here."

The other kids—the girls, Teddy Bear, Action Figure, Hunter, and Teacher—gathered around, crying out, "Is he okay? What happened?" Mommy fell to her knees and clasped Puppy to her chest. As she kissed him and murmured little nonsense words into his hair, she glanced up and saw that Cory was doing the same with Kitty. The two girls stared at each other over the heads of the twins. Between them, the campfire hissed and spit and lit up the darkness around them.

Chapter Seventeen

Teacher sat on the top rail of the fence, watching the horse cropping the grass short in the paddock with Action Figure sitting as still as a stone on its back. Beyond the horse and boy, small white egrets picked their way through the weeds on their delicate, sticklike legs, and from the muddy pond in the center of the field came the soft *plop* of a frog splatting into the water. Already, with the sun up an hour or more, the air hummed with insects and there was a heaviness in the atmosphere that made Teacher squint at the sky and say the word *storm* to herself. She tore the wrapper off a candy bar from the gift shop, inspected it, and took a big bite. It was sweet, and a little dusty tasting.

"By the flippin' flame," Hunter said, leaning against the fence beside her. He unwrapped a candy bar, too. "Where would we be without preservatives? I bet this stuff could last for twenty years."

Mommy was standing beside last night's campfire, snapping together the pieces of a nesting mess kit. "No," she was saying to Teddy Bear and Baby. "You may not have another candy bar for breakfast."

Baby put her hands on her hips. "But, Mommy," she began in a reasonable tone. "Candy bars are good."

"Yeah, but they're not good for you," Mommy said.

Teacher laughed. "You'll never get them to eat

oranges again, now," she called over.

Mommy bit her lip and followed Baby with her eyes as she came over to join Teacher and Hunter at the paddock. "What if they get that disease, curvy? Or is it called crickets? I can't remember."

"Anyway, it's a nice Bonus, just for today," Teacher said. She straddled the fence and watched Cory coming out of the building called Dr. Phineas Shumway's Practice of General Medicine, where the girls had spent the night. Cory was buttoning the shiny brass buttons on her military tunic and stretching her neck first to the left, and then to the right. The golden braid of the epaulettes at her shoulders swayed back and forth as she strode down the plank sidewalk. Doll, Baby, Teddy Bear, and the strays chased after her, their voices high and piping and echoing from the porch overhangs. Angerman stepped out of the photography studio as the group came abreast, and fell into step beside Cory.

"We were talking more about that testing stuff last night," Mommy said, nodding toward Cory with her chin. "I think that Puppy and Kitty are in danger. The Keepers want to steal them from us."

"How can you be sure?" Hunter asked. He turned to check on Action Figure, and seemed to like what he saw. He had a slight smile on his face when he turned back to Teacher and Mommy.

Mommy leaned her crossed arms along the top of the fence. "Why else would the Keepers have come after us?"

"'Cause of Cory?" Hunter asked.

"She wasn't even with us at first," Teacher reminded him. "They came after us right away. As soon as we left."

"Okay, right," Hunter said with a frown. "Maybe they wanted to punish us because Angerman tried to burn down the mall."

The three were silent for a few moments, trying to sort out the logic, while on the far side of the square, Cory and Angerman reappeared with sabers in their hands. They began drilling the younger children, and the parade-ground commands of "by the left, march," and "about face," and "right face," rang out across the dusty plaza. The younger children were confused and muddled but having a good time, bumping into each other as they pretended to be soldiers. When Cory snapped, "present *ARMS*," Baby and Doll and Teddy Bear stood still and held their thin arms straight out, and Puppy and Kitty quickly followed suit. Teacher found herself watching Puppy and Kitty, not wanting to believe what she knew they must all face. Whatever the Keepers' purpose was, Puppy and Kitty were part of that plan. The charioteer hadn't pursued them for revenge—he had pursued them in order to capture the twins.

"Cory's sister died trying to get Puppy and Kitty away from the Keepers," Teacher mused aloud. "And we brought them right back. The Keepers basically stole them from us the moment we got there. We have to protect them now. No matter what."

"We need to make some plans, based on what might happen," Hunter said. He crinkled the candy wrapper in his hand, frowning. "Since chances are the Keepers won't just give up, they might come after us again. So we have to be prepared."

Mommy's face was grim, and she was about to speak,

but the sound of the horse walking toward them turned their heads, and they all looked at Action Figure. Teacher gave the boy a quick once-over with her eyes. Without question, he looked a lot better—just the fact that he was sitting up and taking an interest in the horse was a huge improvement.

"Hey, Action," Hunter said. "Do you think you can drive the chariot yourself if you sit on the horse's back?"

Action Figure's eyes lit up. "Uh-huhn. I c'n do it."

"Because I bet Puppy and Kitty would like to ride in the chariot, especially if you're driving," Hunter continued. "And maybe sometimes you'd have to ride real fast and get the chariot far ahead of us. Like you're winning a race."

"Ya-ya-ya," Action Figure said, nearly breathless with excitement.

Teacher met Mommy's glance and wondered if they were both thinking the same thing. Even under the best conditions, Action Figure wasn't the ideal person to make the key person in a plan. And even though he was much better and getting stronger all the time, he still looked a little bit shaky. His ribs were outlined clearly under the skin of his bare brown chest.

But she had to admit, they were in no position to pick and choose. If the Keepers came after them, the best thing was to get Puppy and Kitty as far away as fast as possible. Action Figure still wasn't strong enough to ride a bike, but he could ride the horse. He'd have to be the driver.

While Cory continued drilling the younger children in the square, Angerman joined the group at the fence and used his saber to hack little chips of wood out of the rails. They sprinkled the ground as he spoke. "So, what's the plan? Stay here and live in the good old days or march onward, ever onward."

"Gonna drive the chair-it," Action Figure said with a proud smile. "Me."

"With Puppy and Kitty riding in it," Mommy explained.

Angerman arched his eyebrows. "Oh, is that so? Now there's a plan that fills me to the brim with confidence."

"It was Hunter's idea, and I agree with him," Mommy said, taking a step closer to Hunter. "I think it's a good plan."

Teacher noticed two odd things at the same time: both Hunter and Angerman went red in the face. Angerman turned away and took another whack at the fence rail with his sword, glaring as if he wanted to chop the fence to bits. Hunter stepped away from Mommy and threw his empty candy wrapper on the ground.

"Come on, Action," he said in a rough voice. "Let's get the chariot hitched up."

Then Teacher noticed a third odd thing: Mommy was looking from Hunter to Angerman and back again with a puzzled look, as if she had just met them both for the first time and was wondering who on earth they were. Teacher itched to write this down in The Book, so that she could study it and figure out what it meant. But she believed—although it broke her heart to admit it—that The Book was closed to her now.

They were delayed getting under way, while Hunter scouted around in a nearby housing development in search of another bicycle for himself. Then, with Action Figure astride the horse, and Puppy and Kitty riding in the chariot, they set out. At first, Hunter stuck close by the chariot, watching to see if Action Figure could handle the horse. But it was soon clear that no help was needed. The horse was amiable enough to follow the lead bicycles, and when necessary, Action Figure made clucking sounds with his tongue to keep the horse moving forward at a steady trotting pace. In the back, Puppy and Kitty stood in the chariot, gripping the bar that ran across the top of it and staring around themselves with obvious pleasure. Puppy let out a bark of laughter when the horse lifted its tail and plopped out a few droppings along the way.

"Why do you suppose they only talk some of the time?" Hunter asked Cory when he found himself riding at her side after their lunch stop. "It doesn't really seem normal."

Cory shrugged. Although everyone else had changed back into their regular clothes before leaving the village, she had chosen to keep her officer's uniform. It was clearly a better choice for her than the wedding dress, in spite of being hot. Sunlight winked on the buttons as she twisted around to look at the chariot.

"Who knows?" she said. "And anyway, what's normal? I know the world didn't always used to be like this," she said, gesturing at a heap of rusted cars clogging a sluggish creek.

"Yeah, you're right." Hunter rode in silence for a moment. Then he said, "Why do you think the Keepers didn't die? In the Great Flame? All the other Grown-ups did. And most of the kids died 'cause there was nobody to take care of them."

A gust of wind threatened to blow Cory's hat off her

head, and she kept one hand on it while she rode. Thick clouds were beginning to mass toward the west. "They always talked about how only the pure of heart would survive for the Second Coming. That the world was cleansed by fire and they came through it unburned because they were good."

Hello, son, my big strong boy, how about a kiss for your old dad? Let me see that test you got an A plus on. Wow! Amazing! You knew all these answers? Good for you! You make me so proud. Give me another kiss—other cheek this time.

"My father was good," Hunter said in a quiet voice.

"So was mine, and he died in a car crash with my mom," Cory said. "Ingrid was good, and she died anyway. So you know what I think?"

Hunter glanced at her, at her fierce, warlike face shadowed by the cavalry hat. "That it doesn't matter if you're good?"

"No. I don't believe that. But if your dad was good, and my sister was good, and millions and millions of other people that died in the Flame were good, then the Keepers were just full of horse turds," Cory said as the wheels of her bicycle squashed through a fresh pile of droppings.

"Yeah, I guess so," Hunter agreed.

He couldn't remember why he had been so eager to be one of the men at the Crossroads, why he had been so quick to believe it was a good place. Now that the whole group of Keepers seemed so peculiar and dangerous to them, it was hard to believe he ever thought they were wonderful. He glanced at Cory: she had been with them since the beginning—or since the end, depending on how you looked at it. He remembered how she had looked when they escaped from the mall, yanking that filmy white veil from her head and letting it sweep away on the wind. Now she looked as if she could lead an army.

Another gust of wind buffeted Hunter from the side. He squinted at the growing clouds. They seemed to boil and swell, bulging outward as they rolled across the sky and covered the sun. The air was cooling off, and dead leaves skittered sideways across the highway.

"Looks like a storm is coming!" he called out to the group. "Better start looking for some kind of place to hide, or we're all gonna get soaked!"

The road climbed a shallow rise, and then off toward the right, beyond a wide plain of marshy grass, there was the ocean glinting like metal. From their higher vantage point, Hunter could see the clouds bunching up as far as the eye could see. Sharp spears of sunlight still sliced down past the clouds onto the water, picking out the faint pale flash of distant whitecaps. The horse's ears twitched forward and back as it trotted on, and its neck was pulled back in a tight arch. Action Figure had his fingers clenched in the mane, and his bare toes hooked into the leather straps of the harness; Hunter saw his brother sway with fatigue.

There had to be something—a motel, an overturned trailer, a rest area—anywhere where they could stop and wait out the storm and gather their strength. A faded and storm-damaged sign read EXIT 51 1 MI. Hunter stood on the pedals as he rode, looking ahead. Then, looking back to see how the others were coming along, he saw something that made his heart leap in his chest.

Behind them, in the distance, something was moving up the highway, moving toward them fast.

Hunter slowed, trying to focus on it.

"What is it?" Cory asked, circling back.

The one moving object separated and became two: two chariots, the horses plunging forward at a gallop.

"Chariots!" he yelled. "Take the next exit. Let's go, let's go!"

Action Figure seemed to be in a daze. He looked around as Hunter sped up.

"Action, go," Hunter said, slapping the horse on the rump. "Puppy, Kitty, hang on!"

At last, Action Figure caught on to what was happening, and he began kicking the horse's sides with his heels as the chariot bounced and rattled along the cracked pavement. A quick glance over his shoulder told Hunter the two chariots were gaining fast, pulled by the white horse and the pale gray horse. Baby and Doll were screaming, and Mommy was trying to herd them ahead of her while Teacher urged Teddy Bear to keep pedaling.

Angerman swung around on his bike, turning to face the onrushing horsemen as lightning crackled up in the clouds.

"What are you doing?" Hunter yelled. He looked for Action Figure: the red horse was just veering off the ramp of the exit, with the bicycles in pursuit. "Angerman, hurry up!"

"Go on!" Angerman shouted. "I'll stall them!"

Torn, Hunter circled again on his bike. The rumble of the chariot wheels was louder, and then drowned in a growl of thunder.

"Go!" Angerman yelled.

"Hunter!" Mommy called. "Help Action! I think he's in trouble!"

Lightning flashed again, and Hunter raced off after his brother.

Chapter Eighteen

The screams of the little ones rose in the air as the two chariots came thundering up the highway. Angerman straddled his bike and planted his feet on either side of the yellow line, standing straight as a sword, trying not to let his fear show. His mind was racing: *I need a plan, I need a plan.* It was one thing to have taken on the Keepers at the bonfire, distracting them with his loony-bin act and swiping The Book from them. It was another thing altogether to take them on here, especially now that they were hell-bent on capturing Puppy and Kitty. How was he going to stall them?

Why don't you ask Hunter-Wunter what to do? He'll know! Bad Guy suggested.

Angerman yanked on the straps of his backpack. "Why don't you shut up? Why don't you shut up for once in your pathetic life?"

Aww, you hurted my feelings! You hurted your poor old—

"Stop it!"

Angerman began humming, to drown out its chatter. He had to focus on what was going on. Over his shoulder, he caught sight of the rest of his family fleeing toward the ocean. Action Figure was barely hanging onto the red horse as they went down the exit ramp.

Hunter and Mommy should have listened to him; they should never have put the boy up on the horse!

Angerman could just make out the twins, swaying and bouncing as they gripped the sides of the lumbering chariot. His chest tightened at the thought of how terrified they must be.

Hunter was racing after them on his bike, although it was hard for him to keep up with the horse. The princess was just behind him, her long gold braid flying in the wind, although she no longer looked like a princess but a soldier, someone not to be messed with. In the rear, Mommy and Teacher were trying to corral the girls and Teddy Bear. The little ones were sobbing, even as their skinny legs were pumping and pedaling like mad, while Mommy wove between them on her bike and shouted "Come on, you're doing great!"

The wind was really picking up, whipping up the marsh grass, whistling through the palm trees. The ocean was black except for the rows and rows of frothy whitecaps.

"And I stood upon the sand of the sea, and saw a beast rise up out of the sea."

"This just in!" Angerman announced in a loud voice. "Today, near Jupiter Beach, eleven children were hunted down by a couple of crazy guys in chariots. 'For the great day of his wrath is come; and who shall be able to stand?' We woulda called nine-one-one, but the phones weren't working. And now for a word from our sponsors!" He rubbed his temples, which had begun to throb with pain.

Showdown on I-95, and I got front row seats. Bad Guy cackled. *Is this fun, or what? Pass the popcorn, willya, son?*

Angerman cradled his head. Why did it hurt so

much? "Surprise that special someone with a Valentine's Day gift from Dayton's Jewelers! And, ladies, if you want to get your whites whiter . . ."

Angerman stopped talking and looked up. He saw that the Keepers' chariots were no longer side by side but one behind the other. They'd had to go single file in order to get around a jackknifed truck with big red words on the side of it: LET US BE THE ONES TO MOVE YOU TO YOUR NEW HOME! The chariot with the white horse was in the lead now, and the chariot with the pale-gray horse was behind.

Angerman stood rooted to his spot and watched the white horse galloping toward him. A hundred feet, seventy-five feet . . . it was getting closer and closer, and yet he couldn't seem to move. *These dogs and cats, they just stand in the middle of the road and see the headlights coming and get hypnotized*, someone said to him once. *That's how Whiskers got killed, and Sparks, too. But you wouldn't remember, you were just a baby then.*

Who told him that? His mother? Angerman closed his eyes for a second, trying to ignore the throbbing in his head, trying to capture the wisp of a memory before it disappeared. If it even *was* a memory. Did he ever have a mother?

Angerman, look out!

It was her voice. Angerman opened his eyes and glanced around. Mommy had stopped her bike and was staring at him. Had she called out to him?

Mommy pointed and said something, but her words were drowned out by a clap of thunder. Angerman turned and saw that the white horse and chariot were almost upon him. He could make out some sort of object in the charioteer's left hand. What was it?

His head hurt, his head hurt, his head hurt. He just wanted to curl up and go to sleep. *"Fear God, and give glory to him; for the hour of his judgment is come,"* Bad Guy whispered in his ear. *"Yea, though I walk through the valley of the shadow of death, I will fear no evil . . ."*

Angerman gripped his bike handles and lifted his eyes to the dark, churning sky. Maybe *that* was the plan. He could throw himself at the white horse, and the chariot would go out of control, and then the second chariot would hit the first chariot. It would be like the pileup outside of Jacksonville: a heap of smashed-up chariots and bones. He thought about Puppy and Kitty, and the other little ones, and Mommy. Maybe it was okay to become bones, if it meant saving your family.

Lightning flashed, turning the black sky pale. A gust of wind blew Angerman's bandanna off his head, and his hair whipped around his face and stung his eyes. The chariot was just twenty feet away now. "We're here with a live report," Angerman whispered.

Um, is this gonna hurt? Bad Guy said.

"'. . . for thou art with me; thy rod and thy staff they comfort me.' Management has announced that fifteen affiliates will be shut down effective tomorrow at nine A.M. This will be our final broadcast. . . . I repeat, this will be our final broadcast. . . ."

A flash of white, hooves, wheels. Angerman squeezed his eyes shut, and waited.

And then his eyes flew open. What was he thinking?

He wasn't done here yet. He had to get to Washington first, he had to find President. Because otherwise, Puppy and Kitty were as good as dead, anyway.

The pounding of the white horse's hooves was almost deafening. Angerman reached for his leather sword belt and grabbed the hilt of his saber. "And now for the news!" he cried out.

The white horse slowed down, and then came to a stop. In that moment, Angerman recognized the charioteer as Daniel 7:15, from the Crossroads.

He also realized that the thing Daniel 7:15 was holding was a hunter's bow.

Hell hath no fury like a Keeper scorned! Bad Guy giggled.

Angerman sucked in a deep breath and drew his saber, and began to pedal as hard as he could toward the horse. But at the same time, Daniel 7:15 hoisted his bow on his shoulders. "Fear God, and give glory to him; for the hour of his judgment is come!" the man shouted. Or was it Bad Guy?

With a cry, Angerman jumped off his bike and rolled on the ground just as he heard the sharp *sssssp* of the arrow whistle by his head. He waited for the second arrow, but there was none. Cracking his leather whip, Daniel 7:15 spurred the white horse forward. The chariot took off in the direction of Action Figure, Puppy, and Kitty as Angerman scrambled to his feet.

"What the . . ."

Lightning flashed again. Bad Guy began laughing. *"Behold a white horse: and he that sat on him had a bow; and a crown was given unto him: and he went forth conquering, and to conquer." Conquering, now THAT is manly stuff!*

Angerman realized that there was no way he could catch up to Daniel 7:15's chariot on foot, or even on his bike. The chariot was going way too fast for him to warn the others. He cupped his hands over his mouth. "The guy's gotta bow!" he shouted.

But the only reply was a clap of thunder. The others had disappeared from view. All he could see was Action Figure's chariot struggling down the ramp. The boy was practically sliding off the horse now. And Daniel 7:15's chariot was closing in, fast.

Just then, there was a flash of gray. Cory was running up the side of the road toward Daniel 7:15's chariot. She waved her arms and yelled something out to him— Angerman could just barely hear the words "Ingrid" and "twins." Daniel 7:15 brought his white horse to a halt, and Cory climbed into the chariot beside him. What was going on?

Before Angerman had a chance to process what was happening, he heard the pounding of hooves behind him. He whirled around and saw the second chariot, the one with the pale-gray horse, coming straight toward him.

The charioteer was Deuteronomy 29:28.

Ooooh, this is getting good! Bad Guy squealed. *"And the remnant were slain with the sword of him that sat upon the horse, which sword proceeded out of his mouth." I'd say this is curtains for you and your little family, wouldn't you, son?*

"No it's not!" Angerman raced over to his silvery-gray bike, which had fallen to the ground, and got back on it. With his right hand, he held the sword aloft while he gripped the handlebars with his left hand. His head throbbing, his heart racing, he raised the saber in the air and started pedaling like mad.

"'And I looked, and behold a pale horse: and his name that sat on him was Death, and Hell followed with him!'" Angerman cried out, charging the oncoming horse.

Deuteronomy 29:28 stared at Angerman wide-eyed and yanked on his reins. But it was too late. Whinnying, the horse reared on his hind legs, lashing out as Angerman swerved out of the way of the deadly hooves. A bolt of lightning ripped through the sky, and the chariot wobbled to the left and came crashing down onto the asphalt. Deuteronomy 29:28 tumbled out of the chariot and landed on the pavement.

Angerman stopped his bike and got off. He walked over to the man, who was lying in the road, clutching his side, a small, bloody stain blooming on his blue shirt.

"This just in!" Angerman announced with a smile. "You Keepers are history."

"Blasphemer," Deuteronomy 29:28 muttered. "Traitor. Sinner. Heathen." With trembling fingers, he reached for the leather holster at his waist and drew out a small knife.

"I wouldn't go there if I were you, Dude-eronomy," Angerman warned.

He raised his saber in the air, poised to slash down across Deuteronomy 29:28's neck.

When Angerman had gone off to take on the white horse and chariot all by himself, Mommy and the others had tried to get the little kids to a safe place. *A safe place*: the words made Mommy want to laugh out loud, like a crazy person. This was not a safe place—there was no such thing as a safe place. They were probably going to die here, Mommy was almost sure of that.

Mommy and Teacher were lying on the wet marsh grass, with Teddy Bear and the girls scrunched up between them. They were all on their bellies, with Mommy holding Baby and Doll, and Teacher holding Teddy Bear and The Book. Mommy could feel rocks and broken seashells and wet grains of sand digging into her bare legs. Their bikes were somewhere—Mommy and Teacher had thrown them into the marsh.

Things were very bad; there was no denying that. The chariot with the white horse had gotten away from Angerman, and was now pursuing Action Figure and the twins down the road. Hunter had ditched his bike and decided to catch up to his brother on foot, by taking a shortcut through the marsh. But Mommy couldn't see him anywhere. Had something happened to him? And where had Cory disappeared to?

The thunder and lightning were very close together now. Lightning, one, two, three, four, thunder. Someone had taught Mommy that once, to count the seconds between them to judge how near the storm was. The skies would be breaking open any minute.

"Mommmmy, are the bad guys gone bye-bye yet?" Baby whimpered.

"Soon, honey, very soon." Mommy glanced at Teacher and mouthed the words: "The Book. Can't you look at The Book?" But Teacher's eyes filled with tears, and she shook her head.

Mommy sighed and propped herself up on her

elbows, to see what was going on above them. She caught sight of Angerman—and gasped.

"What?" Teacher whispered. "What is it, Mommy?"

But Mommy didn't reply. She saw that the second chariot, the one with the pale-gray horse, had overturned. The horse was bucking and whinnying like mad. Angerman was standing over the fallen body of the charioteer, who looked like Deuteronomy 29:28. It was.

Angerman had his Civil War saber raised above Deuteronomy 29:28's neck. It was no play sword—she'd seen him hack pieces of wood out of the fence with it. "Angerman!" Mommy whispered, and scrambled to her feet.

Teddy Bear grabbed her ankle. "Mommy, don't go! Don't leave us!" he sobbed.

"Teddy, it's—"

Then Mommy saw something else. She saw the chariot with the white horse up ahead. It had been pursuing Action Figure's chariot, but now it was standing still. Cory was in the chariot, talking to the charioteer. She was talking and gesturing and pointing to Action Figure's chariot, which was lumbering and struggling toward the ocean. Action Figure looked as though he was about to pass out.

Mommy's blood froze in her veins. Was Cory a traitor, after all? Had the Keepers sent her to keep an eye on Mommy and the others? How could Mommy have trusted her?

Just then, the man raised his bow to his shoulders and pointed his arrow straight at Action Figure. "Noooooooo!" Mommy screamed.

Lightning flashed. Mommy watched as Cory flung

herself at the driver's arm. The two of them struggled for the bow. The arrow flew though the air, and Mommy saw Action Figure's body jerking and slipping sideways off the red horse.

Chapter Nineteen

As Cory struggled for the bow, another crack of thunder tore the sky open. Something hard smacked the top of her head, and then hail was pelting her arms and shoulders. Daniel 7:15 staggered and nearly fell out of the chariot as he tried to protect himself from the blows. Cory wrenched the bow away from him and tried to see what was happening up ahead: the rain and darkness made it impossible until lightning blazed again and lit up the marsh. Everyone appeared frozen in that split second that Cory looked back over her shoulder—Mommy and Teacher crouching on the roadside; Angerman with the sword raised over his head but looking at Mommy; Deuteronomy 29:28 righting the chariot—but then all went dark again before Cory could turn to see Action Figure's chariot or the twins or Hunter. She tried to blink away the dazzle that remained in her eyes, blinding her.

"'And the seven angels which had the seven trumpets prepared themselves to sound,'" Daniel 7:15 shouted, cringing under the pelting ice. "'The first angel sounded, and there followed hail and fire mingled with blood, and they were cast upon the earth.'"

Cory felt a shudder of fear, and she flinched as another flash of lightning flared in her eyes. She tensed herself to jump down from the chariot.

Daniel 7:15 raised his voice, yelling for Deuteronomy 29:28, and then grabbed Cory by the arm. "You're coming with us."

"NO!"

Now that she had the bow, Cory was hindered by it and couldn't turn around to wrench herself free from Daniel 7:15's grip. She tried to bring the bow around to smash him over the head, but it was caught by the side of the chariot. The Keeper yanked the reins, nearly setting the horse back on its haunches. Cory bent to bite his hand where it gripped her arm, but he jerked upward, smacking her in the mouth, and in one quick movement released her arm and grabbed her braid, pulling her head back. Cory's face was turned to the sky, and hail lashed down at her. She tried to breathe and got a mouthful of ice and water.

Choking, she heard the hoofbeats of the silver-gray horse pulling Deuteronomy 29:28's chariot thundering toward them.

"Back! Retreat!" he yelled to Daniel 7:15, the wheels of his chariot skidding as it u-turned across the road.

Cory strained to see through the water that streamed down her face. There was so much noise, so much confusion. From the marsh came screams and muffled yells. Now that the white horse had its footing it began to race, dashing after the gray one, back south. Toward the Crossroads. Cory caught a glimpse of Mommy and Teacher as the chariots dashed past them.

Then, as Daniel 7:15 fought to keep control of the horse, he loosened his grip on Cory, and she flung herself backward, out of the chariot. She hit the ground hard and spun away, rolling down the embankment of the ramp to the highway. Soaked and bleeding, she tried to push herself up, but her arms and legs gave out and she fell facedown into the mud.

There was the owl, waiting for her at the crossroad, its talons gripping the arms of the signpost. It looked down at her, pitiless and proud, and blinked. Then it spread its wings wide. This time the writing seemed clearer, and with each flash of lightning Cory thought she could make out a word here, a letter there. But she was dazed and battered from her fall, and she was too far away to see anything for sure. She tried to crawl closer, but the mud was so slick she kept sliding backward. If she didn't hurry, she knew the owl would close the book and fly off. With a groan, Cory dragged herself up the muddy embankment, cutting her fingers on the sharp grass.

But when she reached the edge of the road, the owl was gone. Another flash of lightning showed her the two chariots disappearing down the highway. Cory gasped, hanging her head like a dog, and then the roaring in her ears got louder and louder and she was falling . . .

When Mommy saw the arrow leave the bow, when she heard the arrow *sssssssssp* through the air toward Action Figure, her mouth opened to scream. But the sound of her cry was drowned out by the boom of thunder that loosed the hailstorm. The next flash of lightning showed the red horse rearing, Action Figure clinging to its neck, and Puppy and Kitty tumbling out of the chariot as it lurched off the road. Then the darkness closed in again.

"Stay here!" she yelled at Baby, Doll, and Teddy Bear. Her voice was harsh with fear.

Teacher was already up, struggling through the heavy sand and grass. Mommy scrambled after her as the chariots of the two Keepers met and then began racing for the highway, with Cory. The sharp edges of the grass sawed at Mommy's bare legs, and her shoes were filled with grit. Someone was screaming, a high-pitched inhuman scream. Action Figure's horse had dragged the chariot onto the beach, where the wet sand dragged at the wheels. Maddened, the horse reared and reared again, trying to free itself from the harness. Action Figure was still hanging on, but he had slipped to one side and was in danger of falling off under the horse's plunging hooves. Mommy saw with a leap of her heart that flecks of blood—whose blood?—were flying into the air each time the horse arched up. Hunter burst out onto the beach yards ahead of Mommy and Teacher. Beyond them, waves crashed onto the beach, and the sand was pockmarked with the pellets of hail.

"Who got shot?" Mommy yelled. "Who's hurt?"

She whirled around. Puppy and Kitty were huddled beneath a clump of sea grape bushes, their arms wrapped around each other. Mommy fell to her knees on the sand in front of them. "Okay, you're okay?"

"The horse," Kitty whimpered.

Mommy looked over her shoulder. Hunter and Teacher were both trying to grab the horse's halter, but the hooves that jabbed the air were too dangerous. Hunter darted in and tried to grab Action Figure but had to fling himself out of harm's way at the last moment. Action Figure was almost all the way up the horse's neck, and he was talking. Mommy cupped her ear to hear over the noise of the storm: Action Figure was talking to the horse.

"Kay, okay, gonna be better, okay," Action Figure said. He was covered with blood, which ran in pink streaks as the rain fell on him. "Don' be ascared no more, don' be ascared."

Hunter and Teacher stood back, rain streaming down their faces and their hands at their sides. Gradually, with Action Figure talking and murmuring reassurances, the horse calmed down. At last it stood without tossing and sidling, its sides dripping with bloody water. Hunter lunged forward as Action Figure fell to the sand.

"Where are you hurt?" Hunter said, raising his voice over the hissing of the rain. He wiped Action Figure's wet hair back from his forehead, and then checked the boy's arms and legs. "Where's the blood coming from?"

Mommy stood, motioning Puppy and Kitty to stay where they were. She gave the chariot a wide berth, and took a cautious step close to the horse. She blinked raindrops out of her eyes and reached out to put a hand on the horse's neck. Its muscles quivered with tension as she felt for a wound.

"Shh," she whispered. She ducked under its chin and looked at the other side. There was a gash along the horse's neck: Action Figure had been hanging off the other side—he must have been trying to avoid the arrow wound.

"It's the horse, Hunter," she called out. "Action isn't cut—it's the horse's blood."

The horse rolled its eyes and jerked its head back as Mommy touched the bleeding cut with her fingertips.

"Don' hurt 'im!" Action Figure cried out. He struggled to get up from the sand, but Hunter held him back.

"I won't hurt him, Action," Mommy said. "But this is a bad cut. We need to get the horse some bandages so he won't bleed so much."

She continued to explore the wound: it was long, but not deep. The arrow must have grazed right across it. Who Daniel had been aiming for was hard to tell, but it was lucky for everyone that the red horse had been moving so fast. Or was it because Cory had been fighting for the bow?

Mommy looked around, straining to see in the dim light and driving rain. Angerman was walking toward them, dragging his sword in the sand, and Baby, Doll, and Teddy Bear were behind him. Far behind them, almost invisible in the murk, was Cory. Even as Mommy watched, Cory staggered and fell to one knee, but then stood and walked doggedly onward.

"We need to find some shelter," Teacher said. She had tucked The Book under her shirt and stood hugging it against herself to keep it dry. "There's some houses up the beach."

Mommy turned and beckoned to Puppy and Kitty, who scampered out from their hiding place and ran to her side. Angerman joined them at the same time, his face haggard. He swayed a bit where he stood, and wrestled Bad Guy out of the backpack and flung it onto the sand. Then he raised the sword over his head and brought it slicing down across the mannequin's neck. With a sweep of his arm, he flung the sword out toward the waves, and it plummeted downward, spearing itself point first in the wet sand. A wave frothed up around it, and then the sword toppled and disappeared.

"And now the news.

"Violent thunderstorms swept up the coast today, putting the fear of God into the unholy and driving them back to their den. The seas turned to blood, and the sky rained fire. In a related story, winter temperatures are expected to be severe this year, as the icy hand of death reaches out for sinners. Shall we dance? 'And I saw the dead, small and great, stand before God; and the books were opened: and another book was open, which is the book of life: and the dead were judged out of those things which were written in the books, according to their works.' Well, we'd better have a look at that book, then, eh? No? Not now? Maybe later then.

"In other news, the peaceful seaside community of Dun Roman Dunes put out the welcome mat for a band of weary travelers today. Sadly, many of the charming cottages had already been swept away by horrorcanes, but the good news is that real estate values inland have skyrocketed—what was once the entrance to the gated community is now oceanfront property. That was a good investment opportunity, wasn't it? Ha-ha.

"Veterinary technicians at nearby Horse Haven report that the wounded steed is recovering well, bandaged by an angel of mercy and put out to pasture.

"Prison officials announced the execution of the inmate known only as Bad Guy went ahead according to plan. However, sources say that it's not over yet, and a Judgment Day is still to come."

Chapter Twenty

Hunter woke with a start and realized that Action Figure wasn't there. The old terror seized his heart—his brother had snuck out again and was stalking panthers and alligators with his bone arra.

But then he heard a wave crashing, smelled the brine in the air, and remembered that they weren't in Lazarus anymore. They were at some house on the ocean, way up north, on their way to Washington. Angerman had found it last night, after the chariots had gone away and Teacher had insisted that the family find shelter from the storm.

He groped around for his glasses and slipped them on. In the darkness, he could just barely make out the others in the living room. Mommy, Baby, and Doll were curved together under a single quilt, snoring softly. Teacher was on a blanket in the corner, with Teddy Bear curled up against her legs. Hunter didn't see The Book anywhere, and wondered about that: Didn't Teacher always sleep with it, to record dreams? Angerman was in a rocking chair, with Bad Guy's head tied to the arm with a length of rope. Angerman was muttering in his sleep: something about mummies or maybe it was about Mommy.

Cory and the wild ones were on the couch. Cory had a white bandage wrapped around her head, from where she'd cut herself trying to save Action Figure. There was no sign of his brother anywhere.

Hunter cursed, and then shoved himself upright.

Where could Action Figure be? He was still sick, and he needed to be resting. Was he sleeping in another room?

In the silence between the waves, the sound of whinnying rose in the air. The red horse, Hunter realized. He stepped over Teacher and Teddy Bear and headed for the back door.

Action Figure and the horse were on the dunes, where grass grew in scattered clumps. The horse was tied by a long rope to a metal flagpole, upon which a faded and frayed American flag flapped in the breeze. Action Figure was stroking the horse's neck and talking quietly to it as it munched grass. Behind them, the dawn cast pink streaks across the gray sky. A sea turtle was dragging itself back toward the breaking waves, leaving a rutted trail in the sand behind it.

Action Figure glanced up when Hunter walked over to them. "Better now," the boy said, stroking the horse.

"That's good," Hunter said. He picked up a pink shell and rubbed the smooth inside with his thumb. "How're *you* feeling? You should be in bed—you need your sleep."

"Better now," Action Figure replied. He held his hand out to the horse, and the horse nuzzled it. Action Figure burst into laughter. "Hey! Tickles!"

Hunter smiled in amazement. Action Figure really *did* look better. The horse seemed to have a healing effect on the boy. "You know," he said after a moment, "I'm real proud of what you did yesterday. Taking care of the horse after that guy shot it with the arrow. You were very brave."

"Brave? Like a man?"

"Yes, like a man," Hunter said. "What you did, that's

what makes a *real* man. Not some stuff in a jar. It's being brave and strong. It's taking care of the things and the people you love."

Action Figure beamed and nodded. Hunter sat down on the sand, pulled his knees up to his chest, and stared out at the ocean. Action Figure sat down next to him. The two of them sat there in silence and watched the sky grow light. Nearby, the embers from last night's campfire hissed and glowed. The horse munched contentedly on a tuft of sea grass.

"We goin' to Wash'ton now?" Action Figure said after a while.

"Yup."

"Bring the horse?" There was a plea in his voice.

Hunter turned to look at his brother. "Yeah. Sure."

The boy's eyes lit up. "Thanks!"

Hunter let out a laugh. "Did you just do Manners, Action?"

The back door creaked open. Mommy poked her head outside. "Hunter? Action? You out there?"

Hunter craned his neck around. "We're here."

"We gotta start thinking about breakfast."

"Okay, no problem. I'll go look for something."

Mommy gave him a smile, then disappeared back inside. Hunter rose to his feet and brushed his sandy hands off against his shorts. "You wanna stay here with the horse?"

"Uh-huh," Action Figure said.

Suddenly, the horse began tugging at its rope and whinnying. "Whassa matter?" Action Figure cried out. The horse sidestepped around, trying to look down the beach.

Hunter realized that the horse was reacting to something. He glanced around. From the south, a dozen horses were galloping through the shallows.

Hunter pointed at the horses. "Look at that, Action."

Action Figure clapped his hands. "Horses! Catchum!"

"They're wild horses. No way we can catch them."

The red horse was whinnying like crazy now. Action Figure stroked its neck. "Whatsa matter? It's okay."

But the red horse seemed to have forgotten Action Figure's existence. It was tugging and pulling at its rope, clearly trying to run to the other horses.

Action Figure turned to Hunter, his eyes filling with tears. "Horse wants to be with 'em."

"I guess so." Hunter smiled at Action Figure, fighting back his own tears. He wished he could help his brother be a man right at this moment, but he realized that there was nothing he could do. Action Figure had to do it on his own.

Action Figure swatted at his eyes with the back of his hand. Then he unbuckled the halter and slipped it off over the horse's head. The horse arched its body and sprinted toward the other horses, spraying sand from its hooves with each stride. Hunter could hardly tell it from the others as the pack galloped down the thin ribbon of beach, heading north into the horizon, as one.

"You wanna come hunt with me?" he asked Action Figure after a minute.

The boy shook his head, his eyes on the horses. "Stay here."

"I'll stay with you, then."

The two boys sat back down on the sand. Hunter wrapped his arm around Action Figure's shoulders. They continued to sit there like that, long after the horses had disappeared from view.

The sun was high and bright as Cory pedaled up the hill, toward the beach. The air smelled fresh and cool from last night's storm, and there were wildflowers everywhere: pink ones, yellow ones, white ones that looked like lace. Except for her two brief trips to East Florida Precision Industrial Lenses, Cory hadn't been away from the Crossroads since the Great Flame. She couldn't even remember the last time she saw a field of pretty flowers or the ocean or a beach.

She laughed out loud. She couldn't remember the last time she did that, either.

"What's the matter?" Teacher called out.

Cory turned around. Teacher had fallen behind and was pedaling hard, trying to catch up.

"Nothing's the matter." Cory slowed down so they were side by side. Teacher's cheeks were red, and she was out of breath. "You wanna take a break or something?"

"No, uh-uh, we should hurry back. They'll all be hungry."

"Yeah, we've been gone a long time."

Cory had Cereos and bottled water in her backpack. Teacher had jars of powdered orange drink and breakfast bars. They had found the supplies at a small market near the highway called Q-something. Cory hadn't been able to read the sign and Teacher hadn't offered the information.

Teacher leaned over her handlebars as they neared the top of the hill. "I hope we got enough food. Hunter usually does the hunting for the family, so I'm not sure how much we're supposed to get."

"He wanted to stay with Action Figure." Cory hesitated. "Are the two of 'em brothers?"

"Uh-huh."

"Wow. And you and Teddy Bear are sister and brother, right?"

"Uh-huh."

"That's nice, isn't it? That you have each other, you know, even after everything."

Teacher didn't reply. Ahead of them, a great blue heron burst out of a clump of palmettos and flew away. She watched it for a moment, and then turned to Cory. "So, um, what are your plans?"

"Plans? What do you mean?"

"I mean, where're you planning on going from here?"

Cory stared at Teacher in surprise. There was something odd in the other girl's expression. Fear, maybe.

"I was kind of planning on going north with you all," Cory said after a while. "To find that President guy. Like Angerman was talking about."

"Oh."

"But even if I didn't want to go north with you all, there's no way I'm leaving Ingrid's . . . there's no way I'm leaving Puppy and Kitty. They're the only family I got left. And plus, my Visioning told me—"

"Yeah, yeah, I know what your Visioning told you."

Teacher sped up, her tires crunching over pebbles and seashells. Cory bit back a cry of protest: *Why don't you like me?* It was an old, familiar feeling, from somewhere deep in her past. She glanced at the pink and yellow and white wildflowers, but she no longer felt like laughing.

They rode up and over the top of the hill in silence. The ocean appeared, brilliant and blue. Seagulls swooped through the air, diving for fish.

Down below, their little beach house sat at the crossroads between the dirt path they were on and another one. The house was almost invisible, so overgrown was it with vines and weeds. Cory thought that it looked like some strange fairy-tale house. Didn't Ingrid used to read fairy tales to her? Hansel and Greggo. Locks and Bears. Little Red Writing Hood.

The girls reached the house and parked their bikes. As Cory walked to the front door, she felt her stomach grumbling. She was used to the regular routine of the Communal Meals. She wasn't used to going hungry or having to hunt for food.

There was no one around. The only sounds were the shush of the surf, the shrieks of the seagulls, and a broken shutter rattling in the breeze. Cory had half expected Baby, Doll, and the other kids to come bursting out, crying: "Whatja get, Princess, whatja get?" Or to see them playing out back, on the beach.

"Guess everyone's inside," Cory said to Teacher.

Teacher popped her kickstand and nodded. "Some of 'em might still be asleep."

Cory let her backpack slide down her arm as she walked through the front door. "Hello?" she called out. Teacher came in behind her, and let the screen door slam shut.

There was no one inside. In the living room, all their quilts, blankets, and other makeshift beds had been folded neatly and stacked in a corner. Doll's one-eyed dolly lay on the floor next to Teddy Bear's red bandanna. A vase of plastic flowers had been knocked off the coffee table.

Teacher swooped over to the bandanna and picked it up. She glanced around, her eyes fierce and watchful as a bird's. "Teddy?"

Cory frowned. "Helloooo! We're back! Anyone home?"

There was no reply. Cory rushed over to a big window in back that overlooked the beach. It was deserted, except for some seagulls picking at an enormous dead crab. Nearby was a pile of black, charred wood, the remnant of last night's bonfire.

She felt Teacher at her side, breathing hard. "They out there? Do you see 'em?"

Cory stared at the bonfire. Fear gripped her insides like a vise.

"The Keepers," she whispered. "Maybe they found this house."

"No way," Teacher said. "'Sides, they only want Puppy and Kitty. They wouldn't a taken everyone." But she didn't sound too sure.

"I guess so." Cory nodded. "Yeah, you're right. Okay, then. Maybe they went for a walk?"

"Maybe. Come on, let's look out back."

The two girls dropped their backpacks on the floor and started for the kitchen door. But as they passed the table, Cory noticed something. The Book was lying there, next to a pineapple-shaped pitcher and a stack of yellowed newspapers.

She stopped and turned to Teacher. "You left your Book? You didn't bring it in your backpack?"

Teacher crossed her arms over her chest. "So what?"

"I thought you always carried it with you."

"That's none of your— Hey, what's *this*?"

Teacher reached over and picked up a pen that was sitting on top of The Book. It was green, with gold words on it.

Cory peered over Teacher's shoulder. "'The . . . W . . . Wo . . .'"

"'The Woods,'" Teacher said briskly. "This isn't my pen."

"Whose is it, then?"

"I don't know. I've never seen it before."

There were some numbers on the pen, too, but the gold had chipped away. "Hey," Cory said all of a sudden. "I bet you Hunter or somebody left us a message in your book. Telling us where they went, I mean."

"No way. Nobody writes in it but me—" Teacher broke off.

"Come on—let's read it and see," Cory pressed.

"No!"

Cory was surprised by the vehemence in Teacher's voice. "Wh-why not?"

Teacher opened her mouth, but didn't speak. Her eyes grew shiny with tears.

"What's the matter?" Cory asked.

"I can't . . . that is . . . I can't read it anymore," Teacher burst out. "Okay? Are you happy? I found a message in The Book about that, and I haven't been able to read it since then."

"Oh."

Cory didn't know what to say to that. Teacher was the owl in her Visioning, and her Book was the owl's book that held the key to Cory's true path. If Teacher couldn't read The Book, what was Cory going to do? And how were they going to find the others? Cory was convinced that one of the older kids had left them a message in The Book.

Cory sighed and glanced out the kitchen window. A wave rolled in and then retreated, leaving a line of dark sand. A dozen sandpipers skittered through the retreating water. Cory thought that she could almost see their tiny wet tracks.

Near the sandpipers, there was a mud-brown pelican preening its feathers. *"I am like a pelican of the wilderness: I am like an owl of the desert."*

Teacher set the pen back on top of The Book. "Come on—let's go outside and look for them."

Cory turned to Teacher. "Grab your Book."

"What?"

"Grab your Book, I have an idea!"

Teacher frowned, then picked up The Book. Her heart racing, Cory ran through the kitchen and living room and out the front door. She glanced back to make sure Teacher was following. Teacher was running, too, with The Book clasped to her chest.

"What are we doing?" Teacher called out.

"You'll see!"

Cory ran past their bikes and across the front yard to the crossroads where the two dirt paths met. She stopped. "Come here, come here, come here," she said to Teacher, almost jumping up and down with excitement.

"What are you doing? We should be looking for the others . . ."

"Just trust me!"

Cory put her hands on Teacher's shoulders, positioning her right in the middle of the crossroads. She closed her eyes, trying to remember how it had been, exactly.

At the crossroads there was a signpost, with arrows pointing down each path, four ways. A great bird, an enormous brown owl, sat clutching the crosspieces with its scaled talons.

"Is this it? Can we go now?" Teacher said impatiently.

"No! Okay, now hold The Book like this."

The owl turned its head slowly, looking down the path to the left, and then turned to look to the right, and then down the path Cory had been trudging along. At last it turned its head back to Cory and spoke.

Cory stepped back, her breath coming in labored gasps now. Teacher frowned at her. "Now open The Book," Cory instructed her.

Teacher shook her head back and forth. "I can't!"

"You have to. It's the only way. Open it real slow, like you're an owl spreading its wings."

"No!"

"Yes."

This is your path, it said, and with an audible rustle of its feathers, spread its wings wide, and it was an open book.

A tear spilled down Teacher's face. Her hands trembling, she grasped the edges of The Book and began opening it with infinite slowness.

A frog hopped across the path between the two girls. A cloud passed over the sun. All of a sudden the world seemed to stand still. Frightened, exhilarated, Cory stepped forward and regarded the open pages of The Book.

There were green words across a white page. Cory reached forward and touched the first letter. *O*. It left a green smudge on her fingertip.

"What does it say? What do you see?" Teacher demanded.

The words revealed themselves to Cory, clear as light. She opened her mouth and read aloud,

"Over the river and through the woods, to grandmother's house we go!"